Break Room

Also by Miye Lee and published by Wildfire:

DALLERGUT DREAM DEPARTMENT STORE

RETURN TO THE DALLERGUT DREAM DEPARTMENT STORE

Break Room

탕비실

Miye Lee

Translated by Sandy Joosun Lee

WILDFIRE

First published in Great Britain in Hardback in 2025 by WILDFIRE,
an imprint of Headline Publishing Group Limited, in arrangement with
O'Fan House, Inc., c/o New River Literary Agency and Danny Hong Agency.

1

Cataloguing in Publication Data is available from the British Library

Hardback ISBN 978 1 0354 3897 6
Trade Paperback ISBN 978 1 0354 3056 7

Typeset in Calluna by CC Book Production

Printed and bound in Great Britain by Clays Ltd, Elcograf S.p.A.

MIX
Paper | Supporting
responsible forestry
FSC
www.fsc.org
FSC® C104740

Headline's policy is to use papers that are natural, renewable and recyclable products and
made from wood grown in sustainable forests. The logging and manufacturing processes
are expected to conform to the environmental regulations of the country of origin.

Headline Publishing Group Limited
An Hachette UK Company
Carmelite House
50 Victoria Embankment
London EC4Y 0DZ

The authorised representative in the EEA is Hachette Ireland,
8 Castlecourt Centre, Dublin 15, D15 XTP3, Ireland
(email: info@hbgi.ie)

www.headline.co.uk
www.hachette.co.uk

Author's Note

Sometimes I say I like or don't like something 'just because'. It's not so much that I feel too lazy to explain – it's more that I feel an emotion so intensely that no further reasoning seems necessary. I actually find myself endearing when I say I like something or someone for no reason. But when I say I dislike something just because, it leaves me with a faint but chilling sense of unease.

Feeling emotions is like digesting food. You want the good ones to settle slowly, to nourish your body and linger. But the bad ones upset your system. They churn and demand to be expelled, that you don't process so much as you vomit. This story is my way of releasing the emotion of 'hatred.'

A break room is a place of rest, but not one where you can stay forever. There are things I need and can use there, but none of them truly belong to me. It's a place for me, except not just for me. In that sense, it's a microcosm of the world we live in, sharing with others.

It's difficult to claim you truly know someone when all you exchange is a passing greeting in the break room. We call that vague dynamic an 'acquaintance.' But even in such fleeting interactions, there are still people who somehow manage to rub others the wrong way and make things awkward, uncomfortable, or tense. *Break Room* is about those people who have never experienced what it means to be genuinely understood, and who make little effort to understand others. Just like how we often treat our so-called acquaintances.

It is one thing to be disliked, but being branded as unlikable without knowing the reason is its own kind of hell. The protagonist is left to endlessly dwell on the question of *why*, turning it over in his mind again and again.

Asking someone 'What do you like about me?' comes with a bit of excitement and a hopeful anticipation that your hunch might be confirmed. But asking the opposite question – I can hardly imagine the dread that might follow.

In this story, the characters react differently upon learning that they're disliked. Some accept it, others have no idea why or simply don't care. And some, despite not wanting to be hated, still somehow manage to make people hate them.

I believe we catch glimpses of ourselves in them, one way or another. They say the only thing we can truly control in life is how we respond to it. So, my way of responding to 'hatred' is to try to imagine being in that person's shoes, and nothing more. But when I do, the raw, volatile emotion that once felt like it needed to be violently expelled begins to settle. The hatred digests into something more bearable – perhaps no more than a faint scowl. But it's one I can live with.

Who is the worst office villain?

A villain who fills the communal **Ice Cube** tray
with cola and coffee?
A villain who owns two dozen **Tumbler**s as a
self-proclaimed environmentalist, but leaves
them unwashed in the shared sink?
A villain who piles used **Paper Cup**s by the
water purifier instead of throwing them away?
A villain who hoards the most popular brand's
Coffee Mix sticks at their desk?
A villain who unplugs the microwave
to charge their wireless **Headphone**s?
A villain who loves to regularly deliver
a **Monologue** in the break room?
A villain who clutters the shared fridge
with **Cake** boxes they never take home?
A villain who **Gargle**s thunderously in
the communal sink every morning?

Now imagine sharing a break room with them.
Who is the biggest villain?

CHAPTER
One

Wikipedia

Break Room

Updated: 202X-XX-XX 20:23:02

Genre: QBS Reality Competition Show / 2023 Release Shows / 2023

This article is about the QBS television series.
For the pantry, see Break Room (pantry).

Overview

Break Room (Korean: 탕비실) is a South Korean reality
competition TV series on QBS created by producer Lee Il-
Kwon. The first season aired every Friday from 10 February
to 17 March 2023. (There was previously a ten-episode
documentary series with the same title that aired in 2022, but
it was discontinued midway through due to low ratings and
controversies surrounding some participants.)

The reality series went viral for its natural portrayal of the participants, and the way it blurred the line between reality and screen by creating the impression that participants were genuinely in a break room instead of on a TV set. As of July 2023, highlight clips of the first season on YouTube average one million views, with the most-watched video being, unexpectedly, a compilation of the participants eating lunch together – it has been described as ideal company for viewers who are dining alone.

Lee Il-Kwon has been engrossed in documentaries since his youth. He thinks they serve two essential roles. One is to reveal the raw, unvarnished faces of human nature that stand in stark contrast to how society wishes to present itself. The other is to expose the truths around us that are often deemed too trivial or uncomfortable to acknowledge. His role model is John Grierson, a Scottish documentary director renowned for the latter approach.

For the original ten-episode documentary series of *Break Room*, Lee Il-Kwon obsessively filmed office workers in the break rooms of real companies or organisations they worked at, meticulously capturing the occasionally villainous behaviours simmering beneath the calm surface. The observational nature of this raw footage alone provided enough material to weave a compelling narrative.

The show revealed the subtle ways in which busybodies tried to eavesdrop on conversations across the room, especially when those conversations involved juicy secrets or gossip. It also documented how many times an employee would come into the break room just to kill time, and what phrases they would most commonly mutter upon entering around 2pm. That show discovered that in break rooms at banks, government offices and hospitals, the most frequently uttered phrase was, 'I want to go home,' while in sales or shipping companies, it was '*Aigoo*, just kill me already.' These statistics quickly became a trending topic online, especially in forums for office workers.

But trouble arose as soon as the second episode aired. A female employee who had seven years of work experience was shown chatting with a coworker when she learned that a new hire's salary was nearly the same as hers. In response, she mixed and drank three sachets of instant coffee immediately, grabbed a handful more, and stuffed them into her pants pocket, walking away with the bulge clearly visible. Her act was captured and broadcast in its entirety, unedited. As a viewer, I loved that scene – it perfectly conveyed how she gave in to her petty feelings when faced with this injustice, and how she couldn't help but take something, anything, from the office to 'fill her pocket'.

But that very scene led to the documentary's downfall. Screenshots of her pocketing the communal office supplies went viral, sparking widespread criticism of the show's approach. Many argued that the ruthless magnification of individuals' private actions bordered on privacy infringement, comparable to hidden-camera schemes – even if filming was done with consent. Unsurprisingly, the harshest critics weren't dedicated viewers like me, but rather people who hadn't even watched a single episode.

Il-Kwon thought of countless past cases where attempts to counter criticism head-on had failed spectacularly, and without a hint of remorse, he chose to change the series format into a reality show with the same title.

The following year, *Break Room* was reborn – not as a meticulously crafted documentary that took months to shoot and produce, but as a reality show filmed over a single week. It became his most notable work.

I happened to be on that reality show. There, I was referred to as 'Ice Cube'.

CHAPTER
Two

It was the first Sunday of December 2022. I remember the winter rain pouring relentlessly, cradled in sleet. I arrived at an office in Seoul to start filming the reality show *Break Room*. I was starving, either from the mouth-watering aroma of egg tarts wafting from a nearby street stall or from the nerves that had made me skip breakfast. I dragged my languid body and a large, tightly packed suitcase that weighed at least thirty kilograms.

I had met the producer Il-Kwon just once, a month before the first shoot. I remember feeling just as famished that day, too nervous to stomach a thing. I had admired his documentary series, and it had never crossed my mind, even in my wildest dreams, that I would be cast in his show – but he had personally selected me.

Il-Kwon was someone who never hesitated to assert

his ideas. He explained that he personally scouted participants, all ordinary people, instead of holding an
open call for auditions. His goal was to find the most
typical office workers he could – and, apparently, my coworkers had put me forward for the role without my
knowledge.

I asked Il-Kwon a series of questions. What exactly had
my coworkers said about me in their recommendation?
What was the specific concept of the show? But he was
quick to avoid all my attempts to grill him, and said that
he couldn't reveal anything until the first day of filming.
All he could tell me was that it would be like a game
of *Mafia* set in an office break room. When he saw the
growing reluctance on my face, he made a bold offer: I
could decide whether to join the show after the orien-
tation event on the first day of filming, during which I
would meet all the other participants. He assured me the
show would merely observe the participants' behaviour,
that the rules were simple, and that filming would only
take a week. To accommodate all the participants, he
had already made an arrangement with their respective
companies for them to continue working from their tem-
porary office spaces on set.

When I told Il-Kwon that I was a fan of his documentary

version of *Break Room*, he seemed pleased, but as he slowly sipped his coffee, I noticed a tinge of melancholy in his expression. After a brief pause, he said, 'Then I have to warn you – brace yourself for a little surprise on the first day.'

The moment I arrived at the filming space on the nineteenth floor, Il-Kwon's warning immediately made sense. The participants were four men, including me, and four women. One of the women was someone I immediately recognised from the documentary series – she was the woman who had stuffed her pockets full of instant coffee sachets after finding out the new hire was being paid the same as her.

The woman glanced around at the cameras set up all over the space, her face sullen as she perched stiffly in a corner. When our eyes met, I offered her a polite smile, secretly amused by her presence, but she dismissed it entirely.

In hindsight, what was the point of all this? Il-Kwon's cryptic comment about me being in for a 'little surprise' had been completely off the mark; it was almost rude. It didn't come close to describing the shock I felt when his production team gathered up all eight of us and announced that they were going to show a presentation based on some surveys they had conducted.

Who is the worst office villain?

A villain who fills the communal **Ice Cube** tray with cola and coffee?

A villain who owns two dozen **Tumbler**s as a self proclaimed environmentalist, but leaves them unwashed in the shared sink?

A villain who piles used **Paper Cup**s by the water purifier instead of throwing them away?

A villain who hoards the most popular brand's **Coffee Mix** sticks at their desk?

A villain who unplugs the microwave to charge their wireless **Headphone**s?

A villain who loves to regularly deliver a **Monologue** in the break room?

A villain who clutters the shared fridge with **Cake** boxes they never take home?

A villain who **Gargle**s thunderously in the communal sink every morning?

Now imagine sharing a break room with them. Who is the biggest villain?

Eight examples and eight contestants – all of us gathered here in the room. I had to read through the examples in the presentation slide before it finally dawned on me: the *Ice Cube* villain in the first line was me. The other participants' faces darkened as the realisation settled in that our flaws had been laid bare for all to see. Our quirky habits – things we'd never thought twice about – were the very reason we were here. The woman from the documentary series seemed particularly shaken; her face twisted in distress as she stiffened and sat upright.

And if that wasn't enough, our expressions – which were transitioning from curiosity to confusion, and finally, to deep embarrassment as the meaning behind the presentation sank in – were being caught on camera. I later discovered that this exact moment was what caused the first spike in the pilot episode's otherwise uneventful viewership graph.

'So, here we are – welcome!' announced the head writer, standing beside Il-Kwon. She looked surprisingly young and wide-eyed for someone in her position. 'We're sorry for the lack of context, but by now, we hope you understand why we had to keep things under wraps, given the nature of the game. Our production team went above and beyond, doing all the legwork and conducting discreet surveys all over the country for a month. We put in quite a bit of effort to ensure you wouldn't find out, just so we could capture your genuine reaction.'

Her cheerful tone was at odds with the shocked and uncomfortable expressions on our faces, as if she hadn't noticed them at all. I couldn't tell whether this was on purpose.

'And now, the results of our survey!' the head writer continued. 'The participant who earned first place received an impressive three thousand, two hundred and ten votes out of a total of twelve thousand, nine hundred and eighty-six. The winner is . . . Monologue!'

She announced it with such genuine enthusiasm that it stirred something inside me. I'd been feeling frozen with shock, but now this was giving way, squirming into an uncomfortable unease.

'As the winner, Monologue will receive a hint card, a crucial advantage in the game.' The head writer paused, then quickly added, 'That is, of course, only if he decides to participate. We've already prepared a filming set and accommodation upstairs for everyone. You're all welcome to stay the night and mull things over, but we'll need your final decision by the morning. Should Monologue decide to forfeit, the benefit will automatically go to the participant who landed in second place.'

'And who the heck is this Monologue you keep referring to?' asked a woman wearing a blue knitted beanie. She was sitting next to the writer.

'Well . . .' The writer paused again. Keeping her tone carefully light, she said, 'How should I put this . . .? We won't be using your real names on the show. Now, I know that might feel a little disappointing – it's not every day you get a chance to be on TV. But above all, we deeply value your privacy as ordinary office workers. So, we've assigned you nicknames based on the descriptions provided.' She pointed at the centre of the slide. 'See here? One of the examples describes someone who murmurs in the break room. That's how we came up with the alias "Monologue".'

Just then, a haggard-looking man across from me started murmuring, swaying slightly as he spoke. 'Wow, geez, so that means I came in first place. And one of you must be Ice Cube, and Tumbler, and Paper Cup and . . . uh, Coffee Mix, too.'

When the man who was nicknamed Monologue mentioned Coffee Mix, I couldn't help but notice the woman from the documentary subtly flinching.

'That's correct, Monologue. Everybody with me?' The writer snapped her fingers theatrically to draw everyone's attention. 'Now, let me walk you through the game rules. Among the eight of you, one person has been planted by the producers. We will refer to this person as "the mole". We will provide you with certain information about each of the participants, but all information about the mole will be fabricated. Over the next few days, your job is to identify the mole by observing each other, using the information we provide and comparing your findings. In other words, you're going to need hints in order to find the mole. On top of that, everyone except the mole will have to play a mind game to try and confuse the others. Remember, you are competing against each other. The fewer winners there are, the higher the prize money! But if none of you identifies the mole at the end of the week, the mole will end up receiving double the prize.'

As the writer rattled off the instructions, I recalled the last *Mafia* game I had played, during a college outing. If the mole was equivalent to the mafia in that game, I was confident I had a chance of winning. Back then, I'd had an uncanny ability, in that brief moment when everyone had their heads down and then simultaneously looked up, to catch the fleeting, mysterious thrills that flickered across the faces of the people who had been assigned the roles of mafia. It was the look of someone who knew they had both the power and the responsibility to steer the entire game.

But there was one thing I failed to account for: that subtle expression wasn't unique to someone hiding a secret. It was almost identical to the face of someone whose vulnerability had been exposed, but who was pretending it didn't matter. At that moment, all eight of us unknowingly wore the same expression – even me.

The fact that Il-Kwon had handpicked and personally scouted for candidates for a game like this, relying on coworkers' referrals instead of holding open-call submissions, pricked every nerve in my body like a needle. It meant that everyone here had been cast because we were disliked – except for the mole.

'Now, shall we go upstairs and take a look around? It's the main stage of our show, *Break Room*. You can leave your belongings here. Our team will take care of them,' the head writer said casually, as though completely oblivious to the tension hanging thick in the air.

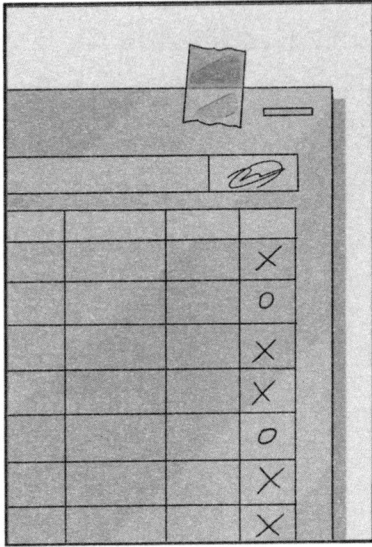

CHAPTER
Three

The upstairs area was fully set up for the show. Though it was just one floor above where we'd been, it felt like stepping into a completely different world. We followed the head writer down a corridor with a stiff, nauseating smell – something like the sharp scent of new textiles. It must be the freshly laid carpet.

The hallway had a total of eight flats, four on each side, the gaps between the doors noticeably wide, hinting that each flat was fairly spacious. Promotional posters of new products from various companies that were sponsoring the show were plastered along the walls. As I walked past one poster of a famous comedian pressing their nose against a vegetable *hobbang* with an exaggeratedly ecstatic expression, I glimpsed a nameplate on a nearby door. It said: 'Ice Cube'.

The documentary woman paused in front of the door labelled 'Coffee Mix'. Her hesitation was evident.

The head writer nudged her to move along. 'We will give you plenty of time to settle into your flats after we show you the break room,' the writer chirped. 'Let's keep moving for now.'

The air on set felt stuffy, making my skin itch beneath my sweater. I took off my nylon jacket and held it, scratching at my chest as I hurried to catch up with the head writer.

At the end of the hallway was a sliding door labelled 'Break Room'. The head writer slid it open in a smooth motion, pushing it all the way to the right, revealing a surprisingly spacious room. It was about 143 square feet – a pretty generous space for a break room. Unlike the stale air in the hallway, the room carried a comforting, familiar scent, like someone had been brewing barley tea or freshly roasted coffee beans.

All the prospective contestants entered the break room cautiously, keeping our distance from each other. Someone flipped a switch, and a waterdrop-shaped ceiling lamp lit up brightly.

The break room was equipped with a high-powered microwave, a compact toaster, a slim yet spotless sink and an adorable ivory-coloured fridge. Three lidless containers sat on the counter, filled with an assortment of snacks, candies and jellies. One container even had mugwort *injeolmi* coated with roasted soybean powder, a brand-new snack so popular that they were rare to find, even at a premium price. Next to the snack containers were neatly organised selections of tea and coffee. The tea selection boasted a renowned UK brand – luxurious and far too pricey for an ordinary office break room – and the coffee offerings ranged from the familiar sachets of instant coffee, a popular everyday option, to trendy experimental options such as zero-sugar protein lattes. Not only that, but there was also a convenient capsule coffee machine, with various coffee capsules neatly arranged by type. But what surprised us most was the famous Italian moka pot and the high-end espresso machine. The large, gleaming silver espresso machine stood like a centrepiece on the countertop, commanding attention and instantly elevating the atmosphere of the break room.

My fellow candidates were silent, but their excitement was obvious. One of them, meticulously groomed from head to toe, leaned in to examine the small toaster with the air of someone inspecting the condition of a vacation home. Earlier, during our meeting in the office downstairs, I'd noticed him checking his own reflection on his phone every few minutes. I'd also spotted an unfortunate smudge of hair wax behind his right ear. For a moment, I considered being friendly and asking for at least his nickname, but then decided against it. After all, what was the point of getting to know anyone when any of us could walk away at any point? It could very well be me.

'Now, everyone, please hold off on exploring until the game officially begins,' the head writer said, subtly tugging at the elbow of the well-groomed candidate, who had lifted the toaster to look underneath it, perhaps already searching for hidden clues planted by the production team.

'You're only allowed to talk to each other in the break room. Did you notice the flats in the hallway? Each of you has a bedroom, a home office and a small bathroom. While you won't be allowed outside during your stay here, the windows will give you some fresh air and will hopefully keep you from feeling too claustrophobic. Please work from your office spaces as you normally would, and you can visit the break room whenever you need a break – just like any other ordinary day at work.'

The head writer's gaze lingered on the well-groomed

candidate, as if keeping an eye on him in case he got distracted or tried anything silly.

'The only rule,' she continued, 'is that you can stay in the break room for up to one hundred minutes per day. Any questions?' She paused, waiting for a response.

Amidst the silence, the ice machine made a clattering noise as fresh cubes dropped into its tray.

'Alright then, if there are no other questions, you can all head to your flats and take some time to decide whether or not to participate in the game.'

But no one moved. Everyone stood frozen, speechless. I was the only one making a sound – my nylon jumper rustling as I tried to keep it from slipping off my arm.

'You said earlier that we need hints to find the mole. How do I get one?' asked a woman with thick, pitch-black eyebrows, breaking the silence with the first meaningful question anyone had asked. Her dark brows made her eyes appear almost grey in contrast.

'Yes,' the writer replied smoothly, 'you earn hints by making certain moves, which will give you a card to trade for a hint. You can then choose one of the other players, and you will receive a hint that reveals something about them.'

'So what moves do we need to make to get those

trading cards?' the woman asked, her thick eyebrows twitching slightly as she frowned.

The head writer's voice shifted, taking on a serious tone. 'You need to break the rules.'

The woman scoffed, her frustration growing. 'But you didn't tell us what those rules are.'

'You'll have to figure them out. That's where the game begins.'

Before anyone could ask more questions, the head writer took a step forward, holding out a black slip of paper she'd pulled from her coat pocket. 'When you get to your flats, you'll find more instructions waiting for you. Please read them carefully.' She began ushering us out of the break room. 'Take the night to think things over, and make up your minds by dawn tomorrow.' She spread her five fingers wide. 'If at least five of you decide to stay, we'll proceed with the shoot!' Then she turned her back on the break room.

As soon as she'd finished speaking, a staff member emerged from each of the eight flat doors, ready to guide us.

'Ice Cube? This way,' called out a young male staff member, gesturing for me to follow.

'Oh, okay,' I replied, surprised by how I'd so readily

accepted being called by my alias instead of my real name.

All eight of us dispersed into our flats as our nicknames were called. The flat next to mine belonged to the documentary woman – Coffee Mix – who had already disappeared inside.

'We've coordinated with your companies so that you can continue working as usual, albeit in a limited fashion,' the staff member explained to me, stepping aside to let me enter the room. 'There's a separate bedroom next to your personal office where you can shower and sleep. If you decide to join the show, please sign this cast agreement and NDA, and hand them in by tomorrow morning.' He handed me a big paper envelope. 'If you choose to leave, please pack your belongings and vacate your flat by dawn. We will be on standby to quietly help coordinate your departure. Have a good night.'

He delivered the instructions with practised professionalism, his tone as polished as though he were reading from a manual. Then, without another word, he softly closed the door behind him, taking care not to make a sound.

I looked around my flat, feeling a strange sense of disorientation, as though some giant had plucked me up and dropped me right into my own workplace. The computer, mouse and keyboard – and even the little snake plant I kept on my desk – were arranged in exactly the same positions as they were in my actual office. Someone had painstakingly recreated every detail, down to the Post-it with my clients' contacts, which was stuck in the very spot where I always left it. The meticulousness of it all was rather impressive.

It was only later that I noticed something unnerving: the workstation wasn't just arranged to replicate my actual desk – it seemed to replicate the precise range of movements I would make when navigating my usual office set-up. The power button was positioned exactly where my hand would normally reach, the desk height aligned perfectly with the angle of my arms as I typed, and even the placement of items in the bottom desk drawer matched up with my hunched-over posture as I attempted to reach them. The realisation sent an uncomfortable chill down my spine.

I tossed the envelope containing the contract on to the desk and walked to the sliding door at the far right end of the wide window. Through the window, I could see an empty park below, softly illuminated by a streetlight that was capturing the falling flurries of snow in a pale halo of light. Everything else outside was eerily still and silent. I gently slid open the door to reveal a small bedroom and a compact bathroom, neatly stocked with essentials. At least they hadn't gone so far as to replicate my actual bedroom. What a relief.

The luggage I'd left downstairs had already been placed beside the bed. I kicked off my shoes and collapsed on top of the covers, still wearing my sweater. Dust from the fabric swirled in the dry air. Now that I was all alone, free from the scrutiny of others, the emotions I'd been burying deep all day began to surface, spiralling uncontrollably.

I pictured the faces of my coworkers. How much fun they must've had referring me for this, all because I put coffee or cola in the ice-cube tray. Did it never occur to them what would happen once I found out? How awkward things would be between us?

I decided then and there: I'd sleep straight through until morning – and then get the heck out of here.

I had no desire to broadcast to the world that I was disliked by my coworkers. What if my family saw it? What if this show created preconceived notions for people who might come to know me? I pictured strangers pointing fingers at me, whispering, 'No wonder people hate him.' The thought deflated me. But soon, a sense of betrayal welled up, slowly brewing into anger – especially towards two of my coworkers, A and B.

A would microwave sauce-covered chicken breasts that splattered all over the microwave, never bothering to clean it up (I even saw him doing push-ups on the floor as he waited for them to heat). B, whose job was stocking office snacks, only bought her own personal favourites.

And yet, somehow, *my* actions are worse than theirs?

If anything, B should have ensured a variety of snacks, both crispy and soft, salty and sweet, to meet the tastes of the entire team: a mix of Moncher Cakes, Lotte Custard Cakes, crackers and potato chips. Instead, she always picked the same old overly crunchy snacks, like *ramyund-dang* and *jjolbyeong*, filling the office with the endless sound of echoing crunches and leaving everyone's fingers covered in seasoning dust. And let's not forget that B, more than anyone else, devoured most of them.

Could it really be that A and B, of all people, had had the audacity to complain to Il-Kwon about me without considering their own actions? Had they really taken such offence at my behaviour? And had this so-called perceptive producer, completely blind to the full context, really cast me as one of the show's 'villains', simply because I dared to put cola in the ice-cube tray?

I couldn't sleep that night. After hours of fretful thinking, I eventually crawled out of bed. It was only natural that my hands would reach for the game instructions and the cast non-disclosure agreement, which I hadn't bothered to look at until now. The NDA was pretty standard: no social media activity for the duration of the production, no unnecessary personal interactions, and strict confidentiality before the show's release.

I set aside the NDA and picked up the game instructions instead. They were much simpler than I'd anticipated.

During the game, you are expected to carry on with your tasks as you normally would do in your workplace.

Work hours are from 9am to 6pm.

You may use the break room at any time but with one caveat: *your time is limited to a maximum of 100 minutes per day.*

Your mission is simple: identify the mole among you.

The mole joined **without a referral**, and every hint about the mole is a lie fabricated for the sake of the programme.

Your goal is to compare the hints provided with

your personal observations to determine who among you is the constructed character.

To get a hint card: Break the 'rules'.

In exchange for each hint card, you can choose which player you would like to receive a hint about.

The hint will be delivered to the wooden box at your door.

I stopped reading and shot up. I didn't remember seeing a box in front of my door earlier. I stepped outside and poked my head into the hallway. Sure enough, eight identical wooden boxes were now hanging on the doors, one for each of us. They must have been set up right after we'd all gone into our rooms.

The boxes were compact, each with a small, hinged door. I opened the latch on mine and found a tiny copper key and lock set inside. Without much thought, I tapped the box lightly with my fingers before using the key and padlock to secure the door shut. My eyes wandered to Coffee Mix's door next to mine – her box was already locked. I returned to my bedroom and turned my attention once more to the game instructions, slowly absorbing each line.

In exchange for each hint card, you can choose which player you would like to receive a hint about.

The hint will be delivered to the wooden box at your door.

Note: *If you want to get a hint about yourself, you will need two hint cards.*

My eyes lingered on the note, which was written in slightly smaller text than the rest of the rules. I hadn't noticed it before. While I was certain I wasn't the mole and didn't actually need a hint about myself, I still wanted to know what that hint could be. The curiosity gnawed at me, far surpassing my desire to win the game or the prize money. I needed to see those hints to know what my coworkers might have said about me. The urge felt stronger than the nervous anticipation of receiving an annual performance review, opening a school report or even reading what people wrote in a farewell card.

My desire to uncover hints about myself was greater than my desire to identify the mole. Giving up and never knowing what my coworkers had said about me felt like a bigger loss. Strangely, as this realisation settled, my chaotic thoughts seemed to fade, leaving my mind unexpectedly clear – like the sky after a storm.

CHAPTER
Four

I woke up early the next day, just before dawn. The clarity I'd felt the night before had subsided, replaced by the nagging thought that I should leave and go back home. But I couldn't bear the thought of facing my co-workers – sulking and picking fights without knowing what they'd said about me, or, worse, behaving awkwardly as if nothing had happened as I sat at my desk.

I wasn't ready to leave. Not yet.

I pulled out the agreement from the envelope and carefully read through the clauses about the prize money and appearance fee. The minimum payout for winning this show, by identifying the mole, was at least thirty million won. If I ended up the sole winner, it could exceed one hundred million. Running the numbers in my head, I felt a surge of enthusiasm. That amount alone wasn't quite enough to fully ignite my motivation from scratch, but it was more than sufficient to push my wavering determination over the edge.

After signing all the required documents, I stuffed myself with the corn soup and warm bread that had been left on the table in my room by the staff that morning (probably a product placement, considering they'd asked to keep the brand labels visible while I ate). Finally, I felt a sense of ease wash over me. As I finished breakfast, Schumann's *Träumerei* played softly through the speakers installed in my room.

It was 8.50am on Monday, ten minutes before the official game was set to begin. It turned out that five participants remained – three men, including myself, and two women. The other three had apparently declined to take part, and were nowhere to be seen.

At the production team's request, we stepped out and stood in front of our doors. I handed in my meticulously signed agreement. In return, they handed out smartphones loaded with only specific apps necessary for the show. I waited for the final instructions before the game officially started.

'This is incredible,' said the man whose flat was in the far corner, diagonally across from mine. It was the well-groomed man from last night, now wearing jeans with a flamboyant flare at the hem. 'How did they manage to recreate my office exactly? Are your offices the same too?' he asked.

By reading the nameplates that had been placed on our doors, I could finally connect each contestant with their nickname. The well-groomed man stood slouched in front of the door labelled 'Tumbler', his pale face glistening under the hallway lights – probably from slathering on excessive amounts of moisturiser the night before.

'Actually, I don't think we've properly introduced ourselves. Nice to meet you – I've been assigned the name Tumbler. What a shame we don't get to reveal our real names.'

'We'll find out in a week,' replied the thick-eyebrowed woman, who was lazily leaning against the door next to him. 'I'm Cake here. I actually like my new name.' Her voice carried a hint of flirtation as she playfully arched her thick, well-defined eyebrows – likely natural, considering the early hour and her otherwise bare face. In complete contrast to her nickname, she was so scrawny it seemed like she'd never deign to touch sugary foods or even taste a single bite of cake.

The layout of the flats suggested that Monologue, who

had been assigned to the flat across from Cake, should be the next to introduce himself, but the winner of the worst villain poll seemed completely indifferent to what was going on. He was handing one staff member a pile of empty breakfast plates he had neatly stacked to make them easier to collect. His face was flushed red as if he'd just finished an intense morning workout.

'The breakfast menu was great. Maybe cornbread next time? I do like milk bread, but . . . would chestnut bread be asking for too much?' he asked, brushing away a stray breadcrumb from under his lips, revealing a lone mole on his chin.

'Duly noted, Monologue,' the staff member replied with an awkward smile.

'By the way, did you know the humidity level in the room is as low as twenty per cent?'

'I'm sorry?'

'Just thought you should know. I actually hate humidity. Still, I'd prefer it to be at least forty-five per cent.' Monologue was almost murmuring to himself. Throughout his monologue, he never once made eye contact with the staff member.

'Well . . . Shall we get you a humidifier?' the staff member reluctantly offered.

46

'Really? That'd be amazing. I won't have to hang a wet towel any more,' Monologue said, clapping softly in excitement.

I watched Monologue, finding myself drawn to the effortless nature he seemed to radiate. I had been observing everyone since yesterday, and he stood out as the only one among us who seemed entirely unbothered by the idea of being on the show. It didn't look like he had bought new clothes for the occasion. It was as if he'd simply grabbed whatever was already in his closet, without giving a second thought to the fact that he was about to appear on TV. His clothes seemed as natural on him as his own skin. In contrast, the rest of us were wearing clothing that carried the telltale rigidity and stiffness of the brand new. Coffee Mix's semi-formal pants were as pristine as freshly laid sawdust, and her dark brown shirt was impeccably smooth, without a single crease or wrinkle.

'I want a humidifier too! Is it first come, first served?' Coffee Mix demanded, shooting one of the staff members an insistent look.

The colours of her outfit reminded me of the layers of instant coffee on top of white creamer powder in a coffee mix packet, and I couldn't help but smile. She caught my glance, her shoulders stiffening as she quickly turned towards one of the staff members.

'I was next! I should get one even if no one else does,' she insisted. There was a strange hint of desperation in her expression.

It struck me that neither Monologue nor Coffee Mix had any intention of introducing themselves.

Breaking the silence, I stepped forward. 'I'm Ice Cube. Looking forward to getting to know you all this week.' I forced myself to smile, knowing that otherwise I might come across as cold. My mouth had a natural droop at the corners, and my face lacked soft, rounded features, so I made an effort to appear warm and approachable.

'Very well, nice to meet you. Some of you are so dry, but I think this'll be fun,' Tumbler said, sounding more like the host than a player. 'Actually, I almost left. I even packed my things, but just before I stepped out of my flat, it hit me – bang! You know, every success story comes with its tribulations. For me, this could be the challenge I need to overcome to make my name known to the world as an environmental activist!' he declared with dramatic flair.

'How about you, Ice Cube? Are you okay going on TV like this?' Cake asked.

I thought her question had many layers to it. The game had already begun, and with just one question, she could learn a lot about me. That meant I didn't necessarily need to answer honestly. If I acted like the mole, I could gain an advantage in the game.

'The mole – whoever it is – is a con artist, hidden among us, pretending to be one of us handpicked villains, and lying to us!' I said. 'Imagine how much fun they must be having. And they even get a prize for it if they win? They're the only one here with nothing to lose. I want to catch this person and get that prize money.'

I deliberately put on a serious face, but the others' attention had already shifted elsewhere. Their eyes were fixed on the elevator, which creaked faintly as it arrived and came to a stop. Out stepped the producer, Lee Il-Kwon. Monologue looked disappointed, as if he had realised that Il-Kwon wasn't carrying a humidifier.

'Now, from this point on, Monday through Friday, you'll all be working as you normally would do on weekdays, while carefully observing each other to identify the mole,' Il-Kwon announced. 'As I mentioned yesterday, Monologue was the winner of the survey and has been awarded a hint card. It has already been delivered to your room,' he added, addressing Monologue, whose flushed face seemed to grow even redder.

'Everyone else, please keep at it. As you know, a hint card will arrive at your door when you "break the rules". You too, Monologue – you'll need to think about what rules there are to break if you want to earn another one.'

'Is that all?' Tumbler asked theatrically, stretching his arms wide and addressing the entire room. 'If we don't figure out the rules, this will only drag on without much progress. I'm sure you didn't set all this up just to film us typing away in our rooms and snacking in the break room.'

'Of course not,' Il-Kwon replied. 'Consider figuring out the answer part of the game. It's the perfect opportunity to observe each other.'

'So, for now, all we can do is blankly watch others. What if no one manages to get a hint?' Coffee Mix asked.

'Oh, I wouldn't worry about that. We're fairly certain that you'll all find them,' Il-Kwon replied, his tone enigmatic.

'That's tricky,' Tumbler muttered in a deliberately lowered voice.

'Also, moving forward, the cameras set up around your designated areas will replace the watchful gaze of our production team, as we take a step back and begin our filming. If you need anything, speak directly to the cameras. Have a great, normal day. Hopefully, one with a bit of fun.'

As Il-Kwon disappeared into the elevator, the hallway was left silent, save for the calming background music that replaced the breakfast playlist. It was that familiar violin arrangement of *Träumerei*, easing the tension and tempering the subtle competitiveness simmering among us.

When the clock struck nine, Monologue headed back to his flat. The rest of us, however, made our way to the break room instead. It felt like everyone was more focused on figuring out how to earn a hint card or watch each other's behaviour than on getting on with their work.

Compared to my quick glance from last night, a closer inspection now revealed just how meticulously the break room had been prepared for the players. The freezer contained an ice-cube tray filled with frozen Coca-Cola, and in the fridge was a large yellow cake box with a Post-it that read: 'Cake's cake. Do not touch.'

There was also a cleaning checklist for the break room attached to the fridge with a magnet, showing all five of our nicknames. We were apparently to take turns completing various tasks, marking each with an 'O' to show it had been completed, or an 'X' if it hadn't. Tumbler spotted the list and immediately pulled it off the fridge, scrutinising it under the fluorescent light as if searching for a hidden message. When the lighting didn't seem sufficient, he casually asked if anyone had a lighter, perhaps intending to hold the sheet over a flame to uncover concealed writing. Fortunately, no one did, and he quickly lost interest, carelessly slapping the list back on to the fridge.

Just then, Monologue appeared in front of the fridge. He had quietly made his way back to the break room without anyone noticing. He grabbed a can of energy drink and a packet of nuts from the snack basket. He seemed visibly uneasy about being in the break room with all of us at once.

'This place is too crowded. The air's too stuffy,' he murmured, gasping heavily as if the room were indeed suffocating. His words, spoken without making eye contact with anyone, were loud enough to sound like a complaint, as though he wanted everyone to hear his 'monologue'.

'All that could be an act, right?' Coffee Mix tilted her head and whispered to me the moment Monologue was out of earshot.

I nodded slightly, agreeing with her. The attributes

we'd been assigned were clearly based upon people's comments from the survey, each distinct enough to make it easy to perform our roles. I doubted whether the production crew would have cast a seasoned actor as the mole. That would've been too obvious; even if no one among us recognised them from another show, someone watching at home might have easily identified the mole from the very first episode, spoiling the entire show. To maintain the mystery, I reasoned, the mole was probably just an ordinary office worker like the rest of us, playing their role diligently to blend in and deceive both us and the viewers.

'I got this tumbler from the very first Starbucks in Seattle. I'll never forget that trip – I got to meet with so many inspiring environmental activists there,' Tumbler said, lining up all the personal tumblers he had brought in next to the sink. There were fifteen in total, each a different size and design.

Every time he spoke, his yellowed teeth stood out even more against his pale complexion. 'When you focus on the big picture, these little trivialities mean nothing,' he added, gesturing towards the cameras placed around the room. 'You know, people get jealous when we aspire to do big things. That's how I ended up here.'

I had to admit, going on a special trip to Seattle just to collect tumblers felt like a big deal.

Tumbler was speaking to me and Coffee Mix, but his eyes kept drifting towards Cake, who was standing by the fridge. She took out her cake, scrutinised it, and placed it back inside.

'Were those cakes for your birthday?' I asked, recalling her characteristic from the survey: *A villain who clutters the shared fridge with **Cake** boxes they never take home.*

'Not necessarily for my birthday, per se,' Cake replied, her voice carrying a mix of defensiveness and regret. 'I keep telling them I'm not comfortable accepting these cakes, but some people always . . . insist. I'll come to work, and out of nowhere, they're forcing these cakes on me. So I end up with a stack of cakes I can't even take home. I know it's a pain for everyone else, but I don't know what else to do.' Her thick eyebrows drooped slightly, adding a hint of guilt to her expression, as if she genuinely felt bad.

'Are you saying the cakes are gifts from your admirers?' Tumbler interjected.

'Oh no, I wouldn't go that far!' Cake waved her hands in a flustered motion.

'No, of course not. It's nothing to fuss over, right? It's just a cake,' Tumbler said, his voice hinting at condescension.

'But if I were them . . .' He paused to clear his throat with a dry cough before adding, 'I'd be more considerate.'

I watched Tumbler with interest. He seemed to be a self-proclaimed environmental activist, with a rather smug attitude that hadn't wavered the whole morning. It struck me that if someone's behaviour felt too one-dimensional, lacking depth or complexity, they might be putting on a performance – and that made them a prime suspect for the mole.

Meanwhile, I started opening every cabinet, big and small, tapping each one to check for hidden compartments. Coffee Mix walked over to a toaster on the counter next to me, holding a slice of bread as if to toast it, though her attention was clearly elsewhere.

'Hey, Ice Cube,' she called out casually.

'Yes?' I responded, trying to keep my tone cool and indifferent, though I was secretly thrilled that she'd chosen to start a conversation with me.

'How about we share anything we find out with each other? Just between us. I think Tumbler and Cake have already made a pact.' Coffee Mix nodded discreetly in Tumbler's direction.

I followed her gaze. Tumbler was shamelessly flirting

with Cake, praising her 'classically beautiful' eyebrows and suggesting she'd look even better on screen if she tied her hair back into a bun, all while subtly trying to touch her face.

'Definitely looks like it,' I agreed.

'So, let's share whatever we find out,' Coffee Mix continued. 'But we shouldn't appear to be too close – we don't want others to suspect us.'

Without waiting for my response, she abruptly walked over to Tumbler, just as Cake exited the break room.

'So, what do you think of her? Cake?' she asked.

'She simply cannot be a liar. I can tell from her face; she has the kind of face that can't hide her true feelings,' Tumbler replied casually.

So as well as being an environmental activist, Tumbler was also a self-proclaimed face-reader. I thought he must either be an expert at sizing up other people in ten seconds flat, or a gullible fool who was ready to accept anything at face value.

I caught Coffee Mix subtly shaking her head at Tumbler from behind. In that moment, it was clear to me – there was no chance of them forming any kind of alliance for the duration of the game.

One hundred minutes per day felt like far too short a

period of time to truly observe much of anything. But the superficial small talk we'd shared had already offered some glimpses into people's personalities. Monologue seemed determined to keep to himself, fitting his nickname perfectly, while Tumbler appeared content, convinced that Cake was all he needed.

That afternoon, I learned something new about Coffee Mix: she lacked patience. It showed not just in her words but in her actions. She admitted she preferred the taste of espresso from the machine but hated waiting for it to brew, so she always chose instant coffee mix with hot water from the tap instead, even though it tasted inferior.

By this point, it seemed everyone had already done a general scan of the space earlier in the morning. Now, in the afternoon, they opted for a strategy of breaking up the remaining time as efficiently as possible, focusing on the areas they had mentally marked to investigate quickly when no one else was around.

I found myself doing the same – listening closely for the sounds of doors opening and closing while working in my office room, waiting for the noise to fade before sneaking around to have a look in the break room. At one point, I ran into Monologue, who was meticulously wiping away ground coffee residue around the espresso machine with a kitchen cloth. He muttered something about despising powdered products as they leave such a mess, but the encounter yielded nothing remotely helpful.

I also noticed some of the small appliances were slightly out of place, as if Tumbler had picked them up again the way he had when we first came to the break room. I lifted them myself to check underneath, but, as expected, found nothing. In the back of my mind, I knew this wasn't an escape room, and such problem-solving methods might not work here, but I couldn't stop the 'what-if' scenarios from spiralling in my head.

Before I knew it, I was on my knees in a rather ridiculous, cat-like pose, craning to peer underneath the fridge. That's when I came face to face with Cake. And in that instant, as our eyes locked, I realised just how outrageous I must have looked. Embarrassed, I jumped to my feet and brushed myself off, pretending that nothing had happened.

On the first day, I found myself going in and out of the break room nearly twenty times, which surprisingly helped me ease into the rhythm of this unfamiliar environment. The power of routine kicked in as I worked through my usual daily tasks, making it feel as though I was simply working from home. The strategically placed cameras, which initially felt intrusive, began to fade into the background. Still, whenever a camera zoomed close enough to catch my face, I couldn't help but subtly tilt my head to highlight my left side, which I considered my better angle.

By 5pm, as the first day drew to a close, everyone looked visibly exhausted. I had skipped lunch but didn't feel hungry at all; I was too preoccupied with hovering around the hallway, trying to save my precious break-room minutes. But all I managed to do was skim through leftover trash bags from late food deliveries that the other players had left out for the production crew to clear away. It seemed many of them had skipped lunch as well, only to cave to hunger and order meals later in the day.

'No, that can't be real. Okay, alright. I'll head back to my flat.'

I heard the commotion from the break room as I stood up, having just finished sifting through the last remnants of the food delivery in front of Monologue's room. It was Coffee Mix, arguing with one of the production staff.

'You have already used up your hundred minutes. You're not allowed in the break room any more today,' the staff member said firmly.

Coffee Mix had been trying to break the only rule we all knew: No more than 100 minutes in the break room. When her time reached 101 minutes, the production crew stepped in and escorted her out.

'How are we supposed to break the rules, then? Isn't this the only rule we have?' Coffee Mix sulked as the staff member dragged her back to her flat. She was right – it was the only explicit rule we'd been given. Or perhaps the hints weren't meant to be earned by breaking such an obviously stated rule. I resolved to keep a close eye on the first player to successfully receive a hint. They would be my primary suspect as the mole. After all, if nobody figured out how to earn the hint, the production crew would probably have to intervene – and the easiest way for them to do that would be through the mole. Yet, as far as I could tell, none of the crew seemed to be taking any action. From other shows I'd watched, I knew production staff often hovered nearby, following the players or sometimes even conducting interviews. But here, they stayed entirely out of sight.

All I could do was focus on my work, working just as diligently as I normally did – if not more so, in order to make up for the extra time I was spending in the break room. At one point, I wondered if this entire show was an elaborate ruse, some bizarre work seminar or sophisticated corporate workshop disguised as a reality show by my company. What a cruel trick that would be!

What was Il-Kwon's game, gathering all of us in this strange place? What exactly was he trying to achieve? I furrowed my brows, replaying his last words in my head, trying to decipher their meaning.

Then, it hit me – I suddenly remembered his response to our last question. Somebody had asked him what he would do if nobody managed to find a hint, and he had replied with calm confidence, 'We're fairly certain that you'll *all* find them,' slightly emphasising the word '*all*'.

What did he mean by that? What made him so confident that all of us would inevitably get a hint card?

That got me thinking – what were the things we were all naturally inclined to do? The habits we defaulted to without even realising it? After all, weren't we brought here because of our notoriously off-putting behaviours, the way we rubbed others the wrong way?

Then it clicked: Il-Kwon's background in documentary filmmaking. Documentary directors went to great lengths to control situations, making them as realistic as possible. If those tendencies still lingered in him, it explained his minimal intervention on the set. Plus, if his goal was to reveal our most unfiltered, discomfiting behaviours, then we were the perfect cast.

So, fine. If that's what he wanted, I'd give it to him.

I headed straight to the break room. My watch read 5.57pm, and the place was empty. I pulled open the heavy fridge door, and a gust of cold air wafted towards me.

Sitting there in the middle was a big, yellow cake box.

The fridge was already exploding with everyone's left-over food from lunch, but the cake box hogged most of the space. The door shelves were crammed with an array of drinks and a chaotic collection of leftover sauce packets from delivery meals. The sheer messiness of it all felt suffocating, like a weight pressing down on my chest. I grabbed the Post-it note stuck on to the box – 'Cake's cake! Do not touch!' – and crumpled it in my fist.

I opened the big yellow box and found, to my surprise, a comically trivial chocolate cake inside, barely the size of my palm. Without bothering to search for a fork, I picked up the cake knife included in the box, hacked off a large chunk, and shoved it straight into my mouth. The heavy chocolate cake – a flavour I didn't usually enjoy – tasted like pure bliss. That's when I knew without a doubt: this had to be it.

CHAPTER
Five

I devoured the cake in a frenzy, finishing it in just under three minutes. It was my way of showing total commitment to breaking the rules, knowing the staff were surely watching from somewhere. And like someone who had never even heard of manners, I left the empty box, smeared messily with cream, right where it was and walked out of the break room.

The act brought back a vivid memory from my childhood, when my older brother brought home an expensive box of chocolates for Valentine's Day. I had sneaked one piece, then another, and before I realised it, I had devoured the entire box. Panicked, I returned the empty box to the fridge and fled to my room. That same reckless, rebellious thrill of mischief came rushing back to me now, just as intoxicating as it had been then.

Sure enough, when I came back to my flat, a golden envelope was waiting for me. It was labelled 'Hint Card'. My theory that breaking tacit, underlying rules in the break room would be the key to getting the hints had proven correct. Excited, I tore open the envelope to find a thick piece of paper. The hint card featured five illustrations: an ice cube, a coffee mix stick, a tumbler, a piece of cake, and a big mouth representing a monologue. Below these drawings, the instructions read:

Please circle the image of the person whose hint you wish to view.

(If you wish to receive a hint about yourself, please submit two hint cards.)

The thought of keeping the hint card till I earned another one and could receive a hint about myself had already vanished from my mind. I was overjoyed by the fact that I had figured out how to get a hint before anyone else. My mind raced ahead, conjuring vivid, Technicolor images of me dominating the game with my strategic thinking, claiming the prize money and basking in glory. Besides, I reasoned, the others would open hints about me sooner or later, and I'd see them when the show aired.

After some thought, I circled the tumbler illustration and slid the card into the box by the door. Within five minutes, I heard a faint knock. I hurried out, but no one was there. Quickly, I unlocked the box with the small key, my eyes darting around to ensure no one was watching. When I opened it, the hint card was gone, replaced by a long, flat object wrapped in golden foil.

I stepped back into my flat and sat at the table, carefully examining the item. It was a chocolate bar, its wrapping paper featuring a caricature of Tumbler's face drawn in black lines, grinning ear to ear; the golden background reminded me of his yellow teeth. Next to his face, in hastily scribbled handwriting, were the words: 'Nutty Chocolate Bar'. It had the unmistakeable look of a hastily crafted prop.

But the most peculiar detail was the back of the wrapper. Instead of a barcode, there was a QR code and a warning label printed in an unusually large font, making it impossible to ignore. Below the QR code was the following message:

Caution: not suitable for those allergic to nuts.

I noticed a thin, peelable film seemed to be covering the first part of the text. Using my fingernail, I scratched away the layer covering the word 'nuts'.

The warning now read:

Caution: not suitable for those allergic to narrow-minded people.

I hadn't expected the hint to come in the form of a warning label like this. But at the same time, it made perfect sense. The fact that the warning label – something typically found on objects – was being used to describe a contestant aligned perfectly with the show's concept of not referring to participants by their real names.

But I couldn't believe this was it. It felt profoundly lacking and vague. Hoping there might be a rolled-up piece of paper or some other hint inside the chocolate, I began carefully unwrapping it and nibbling at it little by little. Aside from the fact that it was incredibly rich and packed with nuts, there was nothing else for me to discover.

Just as I was about to pop the remaining piece into my mouth, my eyes landed on the QR code printed on the packaging again. Then it dawned on me – I still had the smartphone they'd handed out for the game earlier that morning. I quickly grabbed it and unlocked the screen to find only a single app. Launching it made the screen immediately switch to a QR code scanner. Frantically, I tried holding together the torn corner of the QR code I had accidentally ripped off, trying to align the ripped edges as precisely as possible in order to scan it with the phone's camera. After a moment of suspense, a link finally appeared.

I clicked the link and was immediately startled by a loud sound. Panicking, I quickly turned down the volume and pressed the phone to my ear. It was an audio file – a piece of testimony from one of Tumbler's coworkers. The recording was a response to one of the production crew's questions, asking for any anecdotes about Tumbler. The voice was heavily distorted, making it impossible to tell whether it was male or female.

'Oh, you mean that guy who carries around loads of tumblers? When I see him, I think he's a lot like a tumbler himself. You know, all shiny and fancy on the outside – like one of those expensive ones that costs, what, sixty-eight thousand won? But in reality? There's really nothing special about it. Sure, it can keep water warm for a while, but it can't *boil* the water or do anything remarkable. That's exactly what he's like – impressive at first, but once you get to know him, there's really not much to him.' The speaker gave a light chuckle, then lowered their voice. 'And the thing is, he's exactly like a leftover drink that's been sitting inside a tumbler for days. It's stagnant and rotting inside, but sealed shut under the lid. He's so closed-minded and never listens to what anyone else has to say.'

When the recording ended, the room fell silent again. There was something unsettling about hearing a stranger bad-mouthing someone I barely knew. What would Tumbler say if he heard all this? How much of it could he accept? And now that I'd heard it, could I ever really see him in the same light again?

That got me thinking – what would others have to say about me? I imagined a distorted, processed voice describing me. My knees felt weak, and a shiver ran down my spine, sending a cold wave through my veins. The thought was sickening. I could only hope that whatever they had to say wouldn't completely blindside me.

My stomach churned, bloated from the heavy combination of chocolate cake and the nutty chocolate bar I'd just devoured. Queasy, I rubbed my belly and wandered over to the window. Outside, I saw people hurrying along, bundled tightly against the biting cold, their scarves pulled up high, almost covering their faces. Watching those strangers, who had nothing to do with this place, somehow helped me calm down. Slowly, the heaviness inside me began to lift.

At least for now, I held the upper hand. Perhaps, once I'd gathered enough hints, I might be able to afford the luxury of learning what others thought of me.

That night, I drifted off to sleep while gleefully brainstorming disruptive or obnoxious ways that I might break more rules, earning me even more hints. The next morning, I woke up ready to face the day, even without an alarm. I felt unstoppable, fuelled by the confidence that I was ahead of everyone else in the game. By the time official work hours began, I had already checked my emails and cleared my inbox. I was unbothered by even the most tedious requests from auxiliary departments that would normally irritate me. The dozens of cameras scattered around now felt like natural features of the room, like sprinklers and fire alarms.

I finished off the morning's work quickly, determined to get my hands on more hints before anyone else, and headed to the break room a little before 9.20am. But to my surprise, Tumbler and Coffee Mix were already there when I arrived. Tumbler was meticulously rinsing his collection of tumblers under a stream of hot water from the tap, while Coffee Mix was rummaging through the snack cabinet, seemingly lost in her own world.

I opened my mouth to greet them with a casual 'Good morning,' but before I could speak, Tumbler whipped his head around sharply, glaring at Coffee Mix. His dishwashing gloves were still on, dripping water on to the floor.

'I hate to be petty, but how many Couque D'Asse biscuits did you just take?' he asked, pointing at the unmistakeable bulge in Coffee Mix's trouser pocket, from which one of the biscuit wrappers was poking out.

'Why do you care?' Coffee Mix snapped, shoving the packets deeper into the pocket.

'Because there's only one left now,' Tumbler shot back, his tone laced with irritation. 'I think it's Cake's favourite, too. You should leave some for others. They're meant to be shared.'

Coffee Mix suddenly raised her voice. 'I'm sure if we run out, the production team will immediately restock them. What's the big deal? They're paid for with the production budget. These Couque D'Asse biscuits come in boxes of, like, a hundred, and we've barely eaten ten. The production crew didn't buy them individually – they probably got them in bulk. If I don't take them, someone else will.'

As their argument escalated, I quietly moved over to the sink and turned off the tap that Tumbler had left running. The hot water had been running for so long that steam was rising to fill the air and the entire sink was fogged up, with at least ten tumblers scattered inside.

'Who hoards snacks like that in this day and age?' Tumbler retorted. 'Unless there's some deep-seated trauma involved. Seriously, you should ask your parents if there's a heart-wrenching, tearful story about Couque D'Asse from when you were a child or something.' He spoke as if he were genuinely concerned.

'Mind your own business. I know full well about my childhood,' Coffee Mix snapped back.

'Please don't take it personally, Coffee Mix. I only mean well for you,' Tumbler said with exaggerated concern. 'If I were you, I'd see a therapist and get help immediately. Besides, this isn't eco-friendly. You'd be surprised to learn how reckless consumption habits like this impact the planet.' He turned back to the sink, rinsing his smoothie tumbler under the running water. It had a wide opening, large enough to fit his entire fist. He scraped out dried tomato residue from inside.

'Well, maybe you should worry about your own mental health,' said Coffee Mix. 'How rational do you think someone who travels all the way to Seattle, of all places, just to buy a tumbler could be? If the international carbon footprint committee stormed in here with a polar bear, you'd be the one getting whacked on the back of the head with its paw, not me.' She raised both hands like polar bear paws, clearly offended.

I watched anxiously, half expecting her to grab a can of corn from the shelf and swing it at the back of his head.

'That's nonsense! I could spend three whole days talking about how much I've contributed to protecting the environment, but I'll spare you for now. Instead, let me tell you about the tumbler and outdoor cutlery set I recently collaborated on with a big manufacturing company. Want me to send you the link? The materials are top-notch – yes, a bit pricey – but if you use them for, say, thirty years, just imagine how many disposables you'll save. I really should set aside some time to walk you through it. Oh, and we also sell specialised tumbler-cleaning tablets on the website. If you go through the link in the bio of my Instagram account, you can get a twelve per cent discount coup— Wait, where'd she go?'

Coffee Mix was already gone. Watching her leave the

break room, I suddenly realised that hoarding the snacks all to herself was clearly against the unspoken rules. This meant Coffee Mix was almost guaranteed to receive her hint card the moment she returned to her flat. And if she had any sense at all, she'd figure out the entire logic of the game in no time.

As much as I had wanted to savour my momentary triumph – feeling as though I'd won the race, even just for a few hours – I knew this was no longer the case.

'Ice Cube, don't you also think that kind of behaviour is unacceptable?' Tumbler asked, pulling me from my thoughts. 'I mean, sure, it would've been easier to stay quiet, to ignore it. No one likes to be the one who calls someone out. But come on – she can't even hold back when she knows there are cameras rolling. She knows why we're here. I think every group needs someone like me who is not afraid to call it how I see it.'

Tumbler's self-righteous tone made me wince, and he probably noticed my uncomfortable expression. I thought he was being naïve – or had he already forgotten why we were all here? Clearly, we hadn't been brought here to pick at or scold each other. Unless he was the mole, putting on an elaborate act worthy of an Oscar, he seemed utterly clueless about the nature of the game.

Coffee Mix couldn't possibly know that I'd secured the first hint, but I was certain that she'd received hers by now. If her proposed pact to share our discoveries was truly genuine, she would approach me. She might share how she'd earned her hint, or even drop a subtle clue. But although I ran into her three times in the break room as the day went on, she didn't say a word.

That day, I began to detest her. Yet, if I was to uncover the mole, I needed to get to know her better. Never in my life had I tried to genuinely understand someone I despised. *Never.* Hating someone is easy, but making an effort to understand them is hard.

And in that moment, I realised: this wasn't just a game about petty villains in a break room.

CHAPTER
Six

My bedroom's wall was directly exposed to the building's exterior, causing a severe draught that would slowly creep into my office room. As the temperature suddenly dropped, the office room grew increasingly chilly. The only source of warmth came from the hallway leading to the break room and the break room itself. I was often tempted to pause my work and casually wander the hallway. If someone else went into the break room, I'd follow them to quietly observe their activities.

'I cannot wait to see us in the show,' Tumbler murmured to Cake in *banmal*. 'It'll be quite the spectacle, watching how far people are willing to go just to earn one tiny hint slip.'

Cake pressed an index finger to his lips to shush him, which made Tumbler's eyes widen as if he'd just realised his mistake. He frantically glanced around, then let out a nervous chuckle. I pretended not to hear them as I pulled two slices of bread out of the toaster. The edges were completely burnt, blackened to a crisp, and crumbled apart as I held them.

Tumbler and Cake seemed much closer than they had yesterday. They must have spent considerable time alone together to become so intimate suddenly. They were often found whispering to each other or snickering together at their inside jokes, almost as if they were showing off the strength of their alliance to everyone else. I couldn't help but wonder if it was just me, or if the audience would later feel the same second-hand embarrassment I was feeling – it was pathetic.

Despite my earnest hope to stay ahead in the game for at least a day, by Tuesday afternoon, it seemed like everyone had managed to secure at least one hint. The anxious energy that had hovered over their actions the day before had disappeared.

I wondered if Coffee Mix had made a pact with someone else to share hints, but I leaned more towards the likelihood that, like Coffee Mix, everyone else had stumbled upon their hints by chance – or, from the producer's perspective, inevitably, due to our own natural tendencies.

I focused on getting more hints without getting caught, moving cautiously to avoid drawing attention to myself. First, I grabbed Tumbler's prized tumbler – the one he'd bought from the original Starbucks store in Seattle. I filled it with water and drank out of it. I deliberately pressed my lips to the rim, leaving a faint smudge to make it unmistakeable that I had used the tumbler. I tried not to think too much about Tumbler's yellowing teeth as I did so.

Next, I pulled out the ice-cube tray that was filled with half cola and half coffee, and dumped the entire thing into the sink. Naturally, I didn't bother refilling it, leaving whoever came next to deal with the empty tray.

'What are you doing?'

I froze mid-step as I turned to leave the break room; Coffee Mix was standing in the doorway.

'Just came by to check if anyone was here. You know, lounging around,' I said casually.

She walked straight to the fridge and yanked open the freezer. She must have heard the sound of ice cubes clattering into the sink from the hallway – there was no other explanation. I noticed her standing on her tiptoes to take a quick glance at the empty spot where the tray usually sat.

'Oh, I see,' she replied.

*　　*　　*

As I made my way out of there and slid the break room door shut, I heard Coffee Mix humming softly from the other side. It seemed to be her way of saying, '*So, you're not sharing what you've figured out either? Fine. We're even now.*'

When I went back to my flat, I found two hint cards waiting for me in the box. Without a second thought, I circled Coffee Mix on the first card.

Unlike Tumbler's hint, which was delivered on a chocolate bar, Coffee Mix's came in the form of a box containing a set of Swiss army knives. The outer case had a warning that read:

Keep away from children.

As before, I scratched at the surface and revealed the hidden message underneath:

Keep valuable goods away from her.

Judging by the wording alone, it seemed Coffee Mix's greed for communal supplies went beyond mere selfishness – it hinted at kleptomania and warned others to be cautious.

I scanned the QR code on the packaging. Surprisingly,

her coworkers on the audio file speculated about Coffee Mix's psychological insecurities, just as Tumbler did. They were collectively convinced that her hoarding habit must have its roots in childhood trauma or some past incident. Unlike Tumbler, there wasn't a shred of empathy in their voices. Instead, they spoke with a kind of cruel amusement, as though gleefully piecing together fragments of her behaviour into an exaggerated, scandalous story.

Without hesitation, I used the other hint card on Coffee Mix again. I quickly received another Swiss army knife set, but this time, the warning label had changed.

The knife is extremely sharp. Take care not to hurt yourself.

I peeled off the film and the message underneath changed to:

Her personality is extremely sharp. Take care not to hurt yourself.

The accompanying audio hint described an encounter where someone had tried to confront Coffee Mix about her supposed trauma, only to be met with stinging backlash. The confrontation mirrored what I had witnessed earlier between her and Tumbler. Frustration set in – two hint cards wasted, offering nothing new. They merely confirmed what was already apparent: that, at least, I had a fairly good sense of gauging people.

I started to question the authenticity of the audio clips. Were they genuine testimonials from Coffee Mix's coworkers, or had the production crew fabricated any of it to create a narrative? I replayed the recordings over and over, dissecting every inflection and nuance, hoping to detect a telltale sign of a staff member's voice or maybe the producer's recognisable accent. I couldn't tell anything for certain.

By Wednesday, I'd hit a complete mental block. I had exhausted all my ideas for using the existing items in the break room, and it seemed the other players were in the same boat. We all needed to push ourselves beyond our usual behaviours to find new ways to break the 'rules'.

It quickly became clear that the production crew wouldn't reward repeated or similar offences. I confirmed this when I stole a bite from Monologue's leftover sandwich in the fridge, only to find no hint card waiting for me – it was too similar to my first action on day one, when I'd devoured Cake's chocolate cake.

Later, when Coffee Mix left crumbs from her Couque D'Asse snack all over the table, I was inspired to try a new strategy of deliberately spilling juice into the sink. But apparently, that fell into the same category as Coffee Mix's action of 'making a mess', which didn't count.

Fortunately, as the saying goes, yesterday's enemy is today's ally. During this creative block, my biggest inspiration turned out to be none other than my coworkers, A and B. Thinking of A, I microwaved a ready-to-eat mapo tofu rice dish – specifically chosen for its juicy stuffing – and let it heat for far longer than necessary until the sauce splattered everywhere. But even this didn't earn me a hint card, probably because it still fell under the broad category of 'making a mess', like my previous attempts.

However, when I microwaved some *cheonggukjang* I'd ordered for delivery and let the pungent stench of fermented soybeans linger inside the break room by keeping the door shut, I finally received a hint card.

Imagining A and B's reaction when they saw this on the show – and how it might give them something to think about – made me feel more exhilarated than I had since I'd arrived here. For lunch, I treated myself to hot *cheonggukjang* and polished off two full bowls of rice.

This time, I didn't rush to open the hint card. Instead,

I observed what was going on, deciding to wait before using this precious opportunity on someone.

That afternoon, a sudden announcement blared through the speaker system, seemingly prompted by a heated incident in the break room.

'Verbal abuse and violent behaviour directed at specific individuals or groups are strictly prohibited.'

Someone had left the fridge door open, and someone else had retaliated by unplugging the fridge entirely. After a long day of work, eager to savour the GooGoo Cluster ice cream that I'd been saving, I opened the fridge to find a puddle of white and caramel-coloured cream. I was horrified by such cruelty.

By Thursday morning, the madness among the contestants had reached its peak. Coffee Mix stole the spotlight by washing her long hair in the break-room sink. Clumps of hair clogged the drain, leaving Monologue utterly flabbergasted. He stormed off, only to return moments later with a cleaning tool from who knows where, and launched into a full-blown tantrum.

'Dear God, grant me the courage to endure this war . . .' he muttered dramatically, squeezing his eyes shut as he yanked slimy clumps of hair from the drain, the tool gripped tightly in his hand.

As if on cue, Cake barged in and snatched the hot water I'd just boiled, pouring it over her instant noodles without so much as a glance in my direction.

'I'm sorry. I had to do something. I think I'm last,' she said hurriedly.

It didn't take a genius to figure out Tumbler was the one who had talked her into this. He stood nearby, waiting for her, quickly separating and handing her some wooden chopsticks upon her return. His tiny fist shot into the air as if he were a cheerleader and he silently mouthed his encouragement: '*Hwaiting!*'

Had these two been sharing their hints with each other? Or was Tumbler being deceived by Cake, who'd probably exaggerated how far behind she was in the game? Either way, Tumbler seemed to hang on her every word with absolute conviction, as if he were incapable of critical thinking when it came to her. It seemed unlikely that he would have ever thought to question her.

While the rest of us continued playing the game in our own ways, Coffee Mix suddenly let out a loud burp, drawing everyone's attention. For a brief moment, people genuinely pondered whether something as natural as that could count as breaking the rules. But the absurdity didn't end there. Inspired by her act, Tumbler adopted a look of deep contemplation, clearly considering whether farting might count as well.

Before he could put the thought into action, I cut him off sharply. 'Burping, farting and any other bodily functions definitely won't count, because they are basically in the same category of what Coffee Mix has done.' Tumbler seemed to regain his composure and nodded at me in deep gratitude.

With every passing minute potentially altering the course of the game, we all tried to spend as much time in or around the break room as possible, afraid of falling behind in this increasingly competitive environment. Staying in our rooms felt like admitting defeat or indifference. That day, we even decided to have a late lunch together, sitting in the hallway outside the break room.

Our lunch was *bunsik*; Tumbler and Monologue ordered *naengmyeon* despite the freezing winter weather, while Coffee Mix, Cake and I went for *kalguksu*. To share, we got a large plate of vegetable *bibim mandu*. I took charge of calling to place the order at the *bunsik* diner.

When the delivery arrived, the others seemed mildly surprised.

'Extra *danmuji*, and noodles separate from the broth . . .

How did you know my preferences so well?' Tumbler asked, genuinely amazed.

We crouched in front of the break room, unpacking our meals. Cake hesitated for a moment, glancing left and right as though searching for someone to make eye contact with. I quickly dismissed it as just my imagination, but then she spoke up, breaking the silence.

'Ice Cube, you like observing people, huh?' she asked, and then added, with a giggle, 'No, you must really *love* it.' She grabbed her food and started eating, not even waiting for a response.

I was too preoccupied with peeling off the packaging from my meal to say anything anyway.

She giggled again, this time glancing at the others, as if fishing for a reaction. It reminded me of an unpleasant classmate who couldn't stand it when people disagreed with them.

Meanwhile, Tumbler and Monologue were bonding over their shared belief that *naengmyeon* tastes best in winter. It was their first real connection, but it didn't last long. After Monologue carefully cut his *naengmyeon* with the kitchen scissors and, without noticing Tumbler's outstretched hand waiting to take them, dashed into the break room to thoroughly wash them, dry them and place them neatly on the dish rack, Tumbler's expression turned icy.

Rather than getting up to retrieve the scissors for himself, Tumbler widened his mouth and attempted to chew through the stubborn, springy noodles, his yellow teeth on full display as he struggled.

Meanwhile, Coffee Mix tore open the *bibim mandu* container and quickly transferred four *napjak mandu* – thin flat dumplings that looked more like wrappers – on to her plate, while Cake, oblivious, focused on mixing the *bibim* sauce into the vegetables. Then Coffee Mix put the mixed vegetables on a *napjak mandu*, popped it in her mouth, and slyly added another dumpling sheet back on to her plate so that her stash remained the same.

She reminded me of a frantic squirrel, endlessly hoarding acorns, bracing for a long winter or a years-long famine. Pathetic.

After lunch, everyone left the hallway one by one, but I wandered back into the break room and found Cake still there, alone. I felt awkward being alone with her, so I busied myself by brewing a drip coffee, hoping she'd leave soon. The nauseating mix of lingering delivery food smells gradually gave way to the rich aroma of freshly brewed coffee.

Cake stood silently for a while, holding a packet of white tea in one hand and chrysanthemum tea in the other, seemingly lost in thought. Then, as if on a whim, she turned towards me, pulled a coffee mug from the upper cabinet, and held it out.

'Can you share a bit of coffee with me?' she asked.

I blinked, puzzled. Why would she ask to share from the mere twenty drops of coffee I had painstakingly brewed? I was already regretting wasting so much of my precious break-room time – out of the hundred minutes allotted for the day – just on making this single cup. Starting over again for her would be unreasonable.

'Um . . . I'm sorry to say this, but maybe you could make your own coffee instead?' I replied, trying to sound as apologetic as possible.

'Very funny, Ice Cube. You're a very funny guy.' She chuckled, covering her mouth with one hand. But her eyebrows – even more prominent now that her mouth was hidden – didn't seem to match her smile at all. The contrast gave her an unsettling resemblance to someone wearing a *dokkaebi* mask. I couldn't figure out her intentions.

'What is so funny?' I asked.

'Oh, nothing in particular,' she replied. 'It's just . . . Don't you think it's funny? This whole situation. Everything.'

I decided to interpret her interaction as an awkward attempt at reaching out, perhaps looking to form a pact with me, similar to the one she seemed to have with Tumbler.

'Do you want to share hints with me?' I cautiously asked.

'No,' Cake said, shutting down my offer.

I went back to my room and decided to use the hint card I had earned from microwaving *cheonggukjang* on Cake. When I opened the hint box, I found a simple steamed bun wrapped in a transparent plastic wrapper. As expected, Cake's face was printed all over the packaging. The label read:

Shelf life is short as there are no preservatives.

I peeled off the surface film, revealing the hidden message underneath:

The shelf life is short for relationships due to habitual lying.

Curious, I scanned the QR code linked to the hint and played the audio file. The voice on the recording was calm and measured, speaking with a detached yet deliberate tone. It didn't provide specific examples, but instead stated:

'She says a lot about things, but it's hard to understand her intentions. It feels as though she can't stand a situation where she's not the centre of attention. Sometimes, I'd hear her say things and wonder, "Why would she go to such lengths to lie about that?"'

The witness's words lingered in my mind. I moved Cake to the bottom of my list of mole suspects by eighty per cent.

CHAPTER
Seven

Later on Thursday, at 5pm, I returned to the break room. Monologue was meticulously cleaning at the sink. He was stacking the plastic dishes we'd used at lunch, each one now spotless and wiped dry. I quietly stepped in to help him dry the remaining dishes.

'Those are already done,' Monologue said in a neutral tone.

I felt awkward and took a step back. 'Have you got many hints?' I asked, trying to change the subject.

But he said, 'You know that unsettling feeling when you grab the fridge door handle, and it's sticky? People never seem to clean that part.' His words were directed at me, but his eyes remained fixed on the fridge.

'I didn't realise how little we've run into each other in

the break room. How are you doing?' I asked, trying to keep the conversation alive.

'I've made up my mind,' Monologue replied with quiet confidence.

He wasn't exactly answering my question, yet there was something oddly soothing about his presence. His hand, holding the kitchen cloth, worked steadily, without pause, even as he spoke. He moved with precision as he wiped the plates, reaching into every tricky edge and corner. There was a skilful ease to his manner that I couldn't help but marvel at as I watched his meticulousness.

Just then, Coffee Mix walked into the break room. She glanced at us briefly, a flicker of acknowledgement in her eyes, before heading straight to the coffee station. She grabbed five packets of instant coffee and, with practised ease, sliced the tops off all of them at once with a pair of scissors, then dumped their contents into a big paper cup. She poured in hot water and stirred the mixture with a tablespoon, as though she'd perfected this routine countless times before.

She gulped it all down in one go, lumps of undissolved coffee still floating at the bottom of the cup. Without a second thought, she crumpled the cup, coffee dripping from its edges, and tossed it into the trash. The splash left a mess on the lid of the bin, but she didn't seem to care. Instead, she turned to the fridge, scanning its contents for something to snack on.

'Oh my, that dripping mess will make everything sticky . . . not to mention the fridge handle,' Monologue murmured, already heading towards the trash bin to wipe away the coffee stain. He then cleaned the fridge handle twice, muttering about needing a new washcloth before walking out of the break room.

'Did anybody ask for him to do all this? What a show-off,' Coffee Mix complained the moment Monologue was gone. She grabbed the leftover *bibim mandu*, spooning some on to a plate with some tongs, which she tossed carelessly on to the stack of perfectly cleaned plastic plates that Monologue had painstakingly arranged. Red *bibim* sauce dripped from the tongs on to the floor.

Just as the precariously perched tongs clattered loudly to the floor, I turned my back on her and walked out of the break room, flipping off the light switch with a sharp click on my way out.

'Hey! I'm still here!' Coffee Mix snapped.

'Oh, sorry,' I said, feigning innocence. 'It's a habit of mine at home to turn off the lights whenever I leave a room.'

I flicked the light back on, but I couldn't help feeling

satisfied as I returned to my flat. That brief stunned expression on her face was worth it. And then I found a pleasant surprise waiting at my door: a hint card.

I wasn't expecting it, but then I realised – it was the light switch. Turning off the light while someone was still inside the room must have counted as breaking a rule.

After pondering for about ten minutes, I decided to use the hint card on Monologue. Shortly afterwards, a miniature train – something a child would play with – arrived in the box. Beneath it was a disclaimer and a QR code.

Careless use can lead to malfunction.

I carefully peeled off the film as usual, revealing the altered warning:

Careless words and actions can lead to arguments.

I initially thought this could apply to almost anyone here – especially Coffee Mix. But when I played the audio file linked to the QR code, a voice began to testify about Monologue's behaviour:

'Everyone knew there was something odd about him, but we all thought there was no malice behind his actions.

We just figured he was overly focused on his tasks and maybe a little socially awkward. You know the type? There are people like that everywhere. So, I tried to let it slide a few times. But you know what? People like him – they constantly rub you the wrong way, to the point where you start feeling like *you*'re the bad person. It's something you can only truly understand if you've been in that position.'

I threw myself on to the bed without bothering to shower. Did these hints truly lead to a specific person being the mole? Who could even be sure? There *had* to be an answer already; I just needed to focus on reading everyone as objectively as possible. But . . . was that really the right approach?

And what about Monologue? Would he be okay? I found myself reflecting on his decision to stay in the game on the first day, wondering what he might have hoped to achieve through all this. For the first time, I genuinely began to worry about him.

As my thoughts lingered on Monologue with an odd sense of sympathy and my eyes started to close, a sudden announcement blared through the speaker:

'It is now the end of Day Four. So far, the player with the most hints is Monologue.'

I shot up from the bed, wide awake.

CHAPTER
Eight

The announcement had shattered any hope I'd had of sleep for the rest of the night. I paced back and forth in my room, my mind churning with restless thoughts.

From what I'd observed, unfortunately, everyone here *deserved* their place in the game. But who among us was playing their role of being unlikeable so flawlessly? How had Monologue managed to collect the most hints? I had assumed he wasn't taking the game seriously, but I'd been utterly mistaken.

Whenever we'd crossed paths in the break room, Monologue had only remained in the room long enough to quickly complete whatever chore he was in the middle of before leaving. In the countless hours I'd spent meticulously observing the hallway, not once had I seen him act in a way that seemed out of character or remotely suspicious. But what if he had deliberately been using the break room at times when no one else would be around?

I went back to the game rules and read them carefully. Nowhere did it state that the break room could only be accessed during working hours. The rules said we could go there 'at any time'.

Why had I assumed that it was accessible *only* during working hours? In hindsight, it was such an obvious loophole. A glaring oversight on my part. I wondered if anyone else had noticed it – and, if they had, how long had they been exploiting it?

If my calculations were correct, I had twelve minutes left before hitting my 100-minute limit for the day. The thought of returning to the break room felt uncomfortable; perhaps there was a lingering sense of awkwardness from when I'd intentionally turned off the light while Coffee Mix was still in there. But the possibility that there could be something new to uncover late at night or just before dawn, when no one else was around, sent a flutter of excitement through me. It was reminiscent of the thrill I'd felt when I'd received my first hint card.

I changed into clothes that made as little noise as possible, then pressed my ear against the door, straining to catch any sounds of movement. The hallway was silent.

Slowly, I cracked open the door just enough to peek outside. It was dim and eerily still, with no light seeping from under any of the other doors connected to the hallway. It seemed everyone was tucked away in their bedrooms.

I stepped out with my right foot first, crouching low, and began to creep towards the break room. A childhood memory suddenly surfaced: a horror video game I used to play, where my character had to sneak into school the night before Valentine's Day to leave sweets for their crush while dodging the roaming security guard. It was unfortunate timing for the memory to grip me. As if the ghostly presence of that guard from the game had come to life, I could feel something watching me, making my heart pound as if someone were swinging a bat against my chest. Unable to shake the sensation, I broke into a quiet, frantic run, the hallway stretching endlessly in my mind until I finally reached the break room.

The lights were off, and I kept them that way, fearing any beam of light might slip under the door and give me away. My heart felt like it was racing unevenly. The idea of being alone in the break room at night suddenly felt less exhilarating and more unnerving.

The whirling hum of the fridge was oppressively loud. The night seemed to have swallowed not only all the daylight, but all other sounds as well. One cautious step after another, I made my way deeper into the break room, fingers brushing against the cool, metallic edge of the sink as I waited for my eyes to adjust to the darkness. When my hand grazed the door of a cabinet beneath the counter, I instinctively tugged it open. A jolt of fear shot through me at the sight of the deep darkness within. Quickly, I closed the door, turning to the fridge and pulling it open to flood the room with its faint glow.

That's when I heard it – the unmistakeable *squeak* of doors opening in the hallway. Two of them, almost at the same time. Then, two distinct sets of footsteps were making their way towards the break room. Panicking, I flung open the doors of the cabinet once more and squeezed myself inside, shoving aside the random odds and ends cluttering the space. My knees pressed to my chest as I wriggled into a cramped position. I couldn't help but worry that the cabinet might collapse beneath me, silently hoping that the production team had built this set sturdily enough to handle a situation like this. I'd barely managed to pull the cabinet doors closed from the inside when the sound of someone entering the room reached my ears.

A low murmur followed: 'Do you know how much I've

been dying to ask you more about what we were talking about earlier?'

'Really? Well, it's nothing, honestly. What do you want to know?'

'You know what I mean. Who else came to you, and . . . well, *you* know. Don't pretend you don't know what I'm talking about.'

It was Tumbler and Cake. Tumbler's tone was gentle, almost coaxing, except there was a faint edge to it – he sounded slightly offended.

'He came to me wanting to share his hints, but I said no. That's all it was. You know how men flirt – so obvious. But of course, I didn't fall for it,' Cake said, her tone petulant and carrying a smug edge, as though she was used to such attention.

Her words made it sound like another man had tried his luck with her. But wait – there were only two men here besides Tumbler: Monologue and me. And honestly, Monologue didn't strike me as the type to flirt with anyone.

'I knew it! I noticed how Ice Cube kept giving you sly glances,' Tumbler exclaimed, his voice brimming with misplaced conviction.

Unfortunately, Tumbler was wildly off the mark.

'So, why did you turn him down?' he asked.

'Because I don't believe in free favours,' Cake replied smugly. 'There are always strings attached.'

'Of course,' Tumbler said, sounding content. Then he added, 'But just so we're clear – not with me.'

He leaned against the sink, his butt bouncing with barely contained excitement as it tapped against the cabinet door that I was hiding behind. I held my breath even tighter. My knees dug into my chest, and my heart pounded so fiercely I could feel it in my knees. Why hadn't I noticed their late-night rendezvous? Thinking back, they had seemed suspiciously close ever since the second day. Like a couple who'd already spent far too much time together.

How much longer would they stay here? My remaining time was probably already half gone before I'd need to make my escape from the break room.

Through the narrow slit in the cabinet door, I could see their legs. They were standing close to each other, and looked like a strange four-legged creature. I forced myself not to imagine what they might be doing above waist level. Before my mind spiralled further, Tumbler spoke, his tone shifting to something overly serious.

'So . . . who's your pick?'

My ears perked up instantly at the sudden pivot to a meaningful question.

'Will it be that person we discussed before?'

'No,' Cake replied flatly. 'He's not it. He's genuinely . . . off-putting.'

'True. That's not something you can just act out. He probably doesn't even realise he's weird – and never will.'

I thought their conversation about Monologue's quirks had gone a bit too far.

'Exactly. Ice Cube doesn't have a clue; he's probably always like that.'

My thoughts came to a screeching halt. I froze, peering through the thin gap in the cabinet door as Tumbler's legs shifted. He moved towards the electric kettle but stopped midway, turning back to Cake.

'If it's not Ice Cube, then it's settled. If you're certain, I won't argue. Now, enough about the others. How about some tea before bed?'

'Sounds lovely. Thank you,' Cake replied, her voice soft and sultry.

I mentally calculated. At most, I had about three minutes left here, in my hiding spot. A ridiculous scenario played out in my head: if the production crew burst in to drag me out, should I glare at these two for gossiping about me, or sheepishly laugh it off, scratching my head in embarrassment?

My legs, folded uncomfortably in the cramped cabinet, were steadily going numb, a tingling sensation spreading unpleasantly from my toes upwards.

I licked my finger and pressed it on my nose to shake off the pins and needles, and prayed earnestly: *Please, please, let them stop whispering sweet nothings and just go back to their rooms . . .*

'This will be the last time we meet like this in the middle of the night,' Cake said.

'We'll catch up later in the real world, when this is all over. Ah, I'd better head back. My time's almost up. So, we're sticking with the same answer, right?'

'Yeah. Hopefully no one else gets in the way of us winning. I hope it'll be just the two of us.'

A dull thud echoed as a cup settled into the sink, followed by the soft sound of the sliding door opening, then smoothly closing. I held my breath, staying still until the room fell completely silent.

Only then did I crawl out, wincing as I tried to massage my numb legs and feet. My first shaky step threw me off balance, and I stumbled, leaning against the cabinet door. *Crack!* The hinge gave way, leaving the door hanging crookedly. I quickly propped it back into place as best I could, hoping it wouldn't attract suspicion. With my legs still trembling, I tiptoed out of the break room.

Back in my flat, I stopped in my tracks. Two fresh hint cards lay on my desk, as though they'd been waiting for me. My mind spun, trying to connect the dots – the strange conversation I'd just overheard, the insulting comments they'd made about me, and now, the sudden arrival of these hints.

Apparently, I was the first in this game to hide inside a cabinet to eavesdrop – and the first to break the cabinet door in the process. Whether it was the damage itself or my lack of care in attempting to fix it that had raised eyebrows, I wasn't sure. But none of that mattered compared to the fact that I now had two hint cards at my disposal.

I couldn't forget how they'd described me. *Off-putting. He probably doesn't even realise he's weird – and never will.* Without a second thought, I tore open both hint envelopes, circled the ice-cube drawing on each without hesitation, and slipped them into the wooden box outside my door.

Moments later, what I pulled out was unlike any of the previous hints. It was heavier, bulkier. I carried it back to my room, and under the light, I realised what it was:

the wing mirror of a car, detached from its frame. My face stared back at me, and just beneath my reflection, a familiar warning was etched into the surface of the glass:

Objects in the mirror are closer than they appear.

As I carefully peeled away the film covering the letters, the message transformed into something else entirely.

He is watching you more closely than he appears to be.

I stared at my reflection in the mirror. My face was stiff with tension, every muscle betraying the unease I couldn't suppress. The silence was so unsettling that I feared someone else might suddenly pop up in the reflection. An eerie sensation crept over me, and I felt goosebumps prickle along my arms. My hand trembled as I reached for my phone, holding it up to scan the QR code beneath the warning.

I took a deep breath and pressed play on the audio file. The moment the altered voice began to speak, I flinched. I had assumed all previous voices in the hints had been perfectly disguised, but even through the modulation, a familiar voiceprint was undeniable. Despite the altered tone, I knew exactly who it was.

'I'll refer to him as "Ice Cube" here. You mentioned having a slightly creepy encounter with him. Could you tell us more about that?' the production team prompted.

'I'm a big fan of cola. Even at work, I only drink cola. Every morning, I start my day by filling a cup with cola and large ice cubes in the break room and bringing it back to my desk to sip on throughout the day. But, you know, as you drink, the ice melts, and it gets watered down, which is really annoying. I once mumbled this casually, just kind of muttering it to myself at my desk. Then, the next day, Ice Cube – this guy we're talking about – started freezing cola ice cubes in the break-room freezer. Every morning, he'd hand them to me, saying they'd keep my drink from getting diluted. We weren't close or anything, and I didn't want people to get the wrong idea, so it made me a bit uncomfortable. I thanked him, of course. But here's the thing – it became a daily routine. One evening, when I was working late, I happened to notice him alone in the break room. He was pouring cola into an ice tray. And not just any cola – it was the exact brand and flavour I drink. That's what creeped me out. I never left my cans in the fridge. I'd always toss them straight into the trash after pouring my drink into a glass. So I started wondering . . . Was he digging through the trash to figure out what I drink? On top of that, he was spending his own money to make those ice cubes for me every single day. I don't know . . . It just didn't feel right. Especially in this day and age – who does that?'

The witness sighed deeply, then continued:

'And that's not all. There's a coworker who drinks dolce lattes – you know, the ones with condensed milk that supposedly help with digestion? Well, one day, Ice Cube went out and bought another ice tray just to make coffee ice cubes for her. That's when everyone else finally caught on to what I'd been saying. They realised he's just . . . creepy.'

I found it bizarre how they had twisted my small acts of kindness into something sinister. Everyone dislikes how watered-down their drinks get when the ice melts. I'd learned the flavoured-ice-cube trick from my older brother, and since my coworkers didn't have someone like him to show them these things, I'd thought I'd share it by doing it for them, no strings attached. Sure, 1 might've checked the trash a couple of times to figure out their preferences, but it wasn't anything shady. I'd just thought it was more thoughtful to offer silent gestures of consideration than to make a big show of asking.

Making cola ice is easy, but the dolce latte ice cubes? Those took effort. I'd half-freeze the cubes, add sweetened milk midway, and then freeze them again to get the taste just right. It was time-consuming, but I didn't expect anything in return. To me, it was just a thoughtful gesture – an act of goodwill.

Even here in this game, I'd made it a point to pay attention. Walking the hallways, checking delivery bags and noting down preferences for future reference. Didn't they appreciate how happy everyone had been when we had that *bunsik* for lunch? How I'd gone out of my way to order extra *danmuji* and even separated the broth from the noodle? But now, it felt like all the effort I'd put into scouring leftover plates and how much they'd left behind had been entirely for nothing.

I recalled the time I'd jotted down 'hates green peas' after poking through Cake's empty *jjajangmyeon* bowl with a pair of used chopsticks, only to look up and see her standing there. She'd smiled at me, even saying, 'Thanks for your hard work.' (Though, come to think of it, her eyebrows didn't seem to smile with the rest of her face.)

The clock was creeping past midnight, and the world outside was pitch black, with all the streetlamps now off. My reflection in the window stared back. My face was blank, with no emotion. Was it because I was unfazed by all this? Or had the blow from overhearing Tumbler and

Cake's conversation in the break room already numbed me, helping me to regain my composure faster? I couldn't shake that haunting phrase: *He probably doesn't even realise he's weird – and never will.* But I forced myself to gather every rational thought I could, desperate to drown out the unnecessary noise of self-doubt.

Cake had twisted the story to make it seem like I was infatuated with her, offering hints unprompted, when all I'd done was casually suggest we exchange one. Why would she go out of her way to lie about something so easily disproven once the show aired? If her goal was to make Tumbler jealous, she could've mentioned an admirer from the outside world, not a member of the cast. Behaviour like that wouldn't help her win – nor would it help her reputation after this was all over and the show aired.

In the end, wasn't the truly unsettling person the one who tells unnecessary lies for no apparent reason?

CHAPTER
Nine

I couldn't fall asleep that night, of course, and stayed awake until dawn. For reasons I couldn't fully explain, I found myself wanting to talk to Monologue. It wasn't because I suspected him of being the mole, but rather because I felt a faint connection to him – a notion almost pathetically laughable, even to myself. Yet, at that moment, I desperately needed to talk to someone, and he seemed like the right choice.

I was certain that Monologue had figured out long before the rest of us that the break room could be accessed outside working hours, which explained why I rarely saw him there during the day. It was pure speculation on my part that he might drop by early in the morning, but nonetheless, I decided to make my way to the break room at 6am and wait for him.

The break room before dawn felt like an entirely different place, a world apart from its usual self in the light of the day. Over the past few days, everything had always been neatly tidied by the time I arrived in the morning, but now, traces of the previous night still lingered. Tumbler and Cake's cups sat unwashed on the counter, the sink was streaked with dark stains from a soggy rooibos teabag, and while the cabinet I'd hidden in looked fine at first glance, the moment I touched the door, the loose hinge wobbled precariously. Inside, the cleaning supplies I'd knocked over in my frantic scramble to hide were still scattered untidily.

I'd just crouched down to straighten the fallen mould-prevention spray and set the bleach bottles upright when I sensed someone enter the break room behind me. It was now 6.50am.

There stood Monologue, looking refreshed.

'Hey, Monologue, uh . . .' I stammered, my mind racing to find the right words. 'I wanted to talk to you about something. I figured if I came early, I might catch you.'

The words tumbled out before I could organise my thoughts. I forced my sleep-deprived eyes, heavy from the restless night, to look as casual as I sounded – or at least as casual as I was trying to sound.

'Did you open a hint about yourself?'

Monologue's response caught me completely off-guard. I stared at him, blankly processing his unexpected words.

'I'm sorry you did so,' he said. 'But right now, we just gotta do what has to be done.'

He stood on his tiptoes and reached towards the upper cabinets, unlocking a tiny padlock with a key. My eyes widened as I noticed the lock – something I'd never realised was there before. Looking closer, I saw it was identical to those used to secure our hint boxes.

'Why are you using that lock here?' I asked, pointing at it.

'There aren't enough drawers in my room,' Monologue replied simply, pulling out a pair of rubber gloves and a scrubbing brush from the cabinet. Without hesitation, he grabbed more cleaning supplies from the lower cabinet, and began to tidy the break room in earnest.

He tied a green apron around his waist, slipped on the bright pink rubber gloves, and got to work. The rooibos teabag was wrung out and tossed away. The cups were washed and dried. The trash was emptied, and the recyclables were carefully sorted.

It wasn't until I watched him in action that it dawned

on me – every bit of post-filming clean-up I had assumed was handled by the crew had, in fact, been Monologue's work all along.

'Let me help,' I offered, and without a word, Monologue nodded towards a shelf where an extra pair of gloves was neatly placed.

As he wiped down the counter, he suddenly broke the silence. 'It's awful, isn't it? Finding out what people think of you. Normally, we never get to hear these things.'

'I really didn't know,' I replied carefully, each word weighed before leaving my mouth. 'Were you . . . were you aware of these things before you came here? I mean . . . did you know what others think of you?' I added, treading cautiously, unsure if my question might strike a nerve.

'Well, I only recently realised that some people just . . . know. They instinctively understand how they are perceived and what makes others like or dislike them.' His words were as cryptic as ever. He wrung out a wet cloth, gave it a shake, and stretched his back, his face glowing with a genuine sense of satisfaction from having accomplished his routine cleaning.

'Is that why you do all this?' I asked, summoning my courage. 'To try and get along with people?'

He stopped and looked at me, a faint flicker of surprise

in his eyes. 'With just this?' he asked. He shook his head. 'Once you've lost too many points, no amount of extra points will ever help you catch up.'

After that, the details of our conversation blurred in my memory, mostly because my mind had begun spinning out of control. All I could recall was a single, unrelenting thought echoing in my head: *This person must have been made up for the show. He must be a created character.*

I let Monologue continue speaking, his words washing over me as I constructed an image of him: someone slightly detached from reality, a man who interacted with others in an overly precise, almost unnatural way.

Eventually, I decided to push the entire conversation out of my mind, settling on one conclusion: Monologue *had* to be the mole.

Only then did I feel the beginnings of a fragile peace. The desire I'd once had for Monologue to be stranger than me shifted, and I began to wish he was entirely ordinary. I wanted everyone here to be utterly blind to the truth; I wanted the people who'd labelled us both as strange to be the truly odd ones. Then, maybe, I could be the normal one. I felt like a piece on an *Othello* board, flipping endlessly between black and white as my perceptions of the people around me shifted with every interaction.

Monologue finished cleaning and moved to the narrow space between the fridge and the wall, reaching for something hidden there. To my surprise, it was the cleaning checklist, the one that had been on the fridge door on the first day. Tumbler had examined it, flipping it over and holding it up to the light as if it might hold a secret. Apparently, Monologue had tucked it away here, out of sight.

From his apron packet, Monologue pulled out a thick pen and began marking the checklist with rapid, deliberate strokes. I glanced at the sheet from the side and was engulfed by an icy wave of unease – it was covered entirely in X marks. Why? What did it mean? Why would someone go to the trouble of marking every single task with an X?

I realised Monologue was crossing out the boxes next to everyone's name except his own; these, he had filled with bold circles. I felt his pen pressed harder against the paper when he marked the others' names with an X – though perhaps that was just my imagination. I almost asked, 'Wouldn't most people ask others to help with cleaning, or at least leave the boxes of those who didn't help blank rather than marking them with crosses?'

As if reading my mind, Monologue stopped mid-mark and turned towards me.

'Oh, almost forgot!' he said lightly, flashing a quick smile. And he changed a few of the Xs next to my name for today's cleaning tasks into Os. At that moment, I felt as though I was watching the exact mechanism by which he had gradually alienated himself from others – through these subtle, almost imperceptible misunderstandings. The sincerity in his movements, juxtaposed with the unintended missteps that betrayed his intentions, left no room for doubt in my mind.

I instinctively knew – there was no way this was an act.

Yet, when Friday evening arrived, and it was time to officially submit my guess for the mole, I wrote down Monologue as my final answer, after much internal debate.

Still, a quiet, desperate thought lingered in the back of my mind: I wished that someone – anyone – would pick me as the mole. Just once, I wanted to be seen as something other than 'the weird one'.

CHAPTER
Ten

To reveal the underwhelming ending: the mole turned out to be Cake, and only two people guessed correctly – Tumbler and Coffee Mix. I had a fleeting curiosity about why Tumbler and Cake hadn't submitted the same answer, but with filming wrapped, it no longer seemed to matter.

Two months later, *Break Room* began airing every Friday night at 10pm. Watching myself on screen felt strange – uncomfortable, even – but to my surprise, I actually enjoyed the show. Seeing the events from an outsider's perspective, complete with footage of what had happened behind my back, was surreal. They say the closer you are to something, the harder it is to see the full picture, and I could have never anticipated the show would come together as it did.

What stood out most was a segment featuring Coffee

Mix's parents, their faces fully revealed in a video interview. They spoke warmly about their daughter, emphasising how they'd always supported her emotionally and financially. Her 'mild collecting tendencies', as they called them, had started as early as elementary school, but they adamantly denied any association to some deep underlying trauma.

After the interview, what followed was a comedic montage highlighting Coffee Mix's minor hoarding habits. The editors played up the humour, cutting together clips of her collecting small items up to ten times a day, set to upbeat background music. They were cleverly juxtaposed with deadpan interviews from family and friends throwing around jargon in an effort to explain her behaviour. The absurd contrast, combined with shots of Coffee Mix blissfully sipping coffee or munching on snacks, turned the segment into unintentional comedy gold.

Meanwhile, Tumbler, early in the game, leaned into the camera and whispered with conviction that Cake didn't have 'the face of someone who can't hide her true feelings', but instead 'the face of a master deceiver'. (This moment was cleverly highlighted as a teaser for episode two.) With great fervour, he launched into an analysis of the facial features and expressions of so-called environmental activists who seek investments under the pretence of eco-friendly ventures but are, in truth, dishonest. In a heated tirade to the camera, he listed all the reasons why Cake had to be the mole, pointing to her facial features as 'evidence' – features that, amusingly, bore a striking resemblance to his own. The editors didn't miss the comedic opportunity, juxtaposing close-ups of Tumbler and Cake side by side, adding a dose of irony and perfectly breaking the tension.

Despite correctly identifying Cake as the mole quite early on, Tumbler played the game skilfully. He put on a false front when interacting with her, even scheming to cast a fake vote for Coffee Mix to throw her off the scent. From the start, his personal interest in Cake appeared non-existent, and – whether fortunately or unfortunately – it seemed the feeling was mutual.

The show also revealed how Monologue had accumulated hints: he had been stashing personal cleaning supplies in the break room's communal cabinets, and throwing away leftover food that others had saved for later, presumably to reduce clutter or as part of his cleaning routine. (Whether these actions were intentional or unintentional remained unclear.)

One of the most-debated elements of the show

became Monologue's cleaning checklist. Online forums exploded with discussions about whether it was fair for him to have earned a hint card by marking Xs next to the other players' names to imply they hadn't fulfilled their cleaning duties.

Some viewers argued: 'If he cleaned, marking an O for his own name would've been enough. Crossing off others feels passive-aggressive – it's basic social etiquette to avoid unnecessary conflict.'

Others countered: 'It's just a system to show who cleaned and who didn't. If the checklist offends you, maybe you should be cast in the next season of the show!'

Beyond that, the scenes of each player revealing their pick for the mole were cleverly edited, intercut with flashbacks of their actions leading up to their choices, and revisiting key moments throughout the duration of filming to show how each person came to their own conclusion, adding an extra layer of fun.

The inner turmoil I'd experienced while filming didn't make it on to the screen at all. There were brief shots of my face that captured fragments of my emotions, but my distress had clearly been overlooked by the editor, leaving me relegated to the background – little more than part of the set-dressing.

I was grateful that my internal struggles weren't visible on screen, yet I couldn't help but wonder whether, in all the reality shows I'd watched in the past, had I ever truly seen the truth of what was happening? Or was I only ever seeing what someone had wanted me to see?

After the success of *Break Room* and the buzz surrounding the show, my coworkers started coming up to me, saying how much they'd enjoyed the show and offering their apologies for nominating me. They claimed they had 'misunderstood' me. I almost wanted to respond, 'That's not what we call "misunderstanding",' but I held my tongue. Instead, I told them I'd been inspired by the antics of A and B, which had helped me earn the hint cards – a line I thought was a good joke. But they didn't laugh.

I wasn't sure which moment made me feel more pathetic – when my joke fell flat, or when I watched Monologue in the final episode, writing his own name on the answer sheet and muttering, 'I'm enough as I am,' as though trying to console himself.

A few months after the show aired, rumours began swirling that the production team had already begun their recruitment process for contestants for season two. In the meantime, a mobile game based on *Break Room* was under development, with a release date fast approaching. Social media was buzzing with posts looking for beta testers:

We're hiring beta testers for the game *Break Room*!

Find the mole, make a mess in the break room and complete secret missions that only open at night.

What kind of villains have you met in your break room?

Leave a comment and receive a gift package worth 30,000 won!

Curious, I clicked on the post and saw more than five thousand comments, with each person boasting about their worst break-room villains. There was a villain who froze doughnuts only to abandon them to their frosty doom, a villain who left rotten salad in the fridge, and a villain who brought their blender to work every morning to make ABC juice (the blender being a compromise, apparently, as they'd started out bringing in a full-sized juicer). Others called out break-room supply managers who stocked only the most unpopular snacks, or hoarders, or those who emptied the ice-cube tray the moment it refilled. The list was endless.

As I read further, the tone shifted. What had started as light-hearted complaints turned into bleak reflections:

'There's no hope for humankind.'

'What happened to decency?'

One commenter even wrote a long op-ed on cancel culture in modern society. Others spiralled into outright inflammatory rants.

I switched the sorting order from *newest* to *most liked*, and saw a lengthy comment with more than 2,000 likes at the top:

'This is a bit off-topic, but... Do you guys remember the player Cake from season one? The mole? She used to work at our company. She didn't actually leave cakes in the fridge, but she did bring them to the office often. She'd always brag about guys buying them for her. One day, though, I saw her at a bakery far from the office, buying the cake herself. That's when I started keeping my distance. Later, I heard she'd moved to another company. Seems like she's not pulling stunts there. I don't know how much the producers knew when they cast her, but seeing her as the mole gave me the chills.'

Reading the comment, I found myself thinking about the producer, Lee Il-Kwon, whose face I hadn't seen since the shoot. For a brief moment, I struggled to dissociate the unease from the memory of his silhouette. But I couldn't shake the sense that a producer whose work thrives on capturing the unsettling might still be orchestrating something long after the cameras have stopped rolling.

I felt as if his documentary was still unfolding; it had expanded beyond the original cast and was now set in the real world. A more expansive backdrop than his debut work, and infinitely more disquieting.

After all, with a world full of disagreeable people, he'd never run out of content – or villains.

Translator's Note

As an office worker-translator myself, I might've had a little too much fun translating this thrilling, delightfully sharp story about . . . office workers. If you know anything about office life, you'll understand just how ironic that sounds. 'Thrilling' isn't exactly a word we associate with corporate cubicles and break rooms.

But that's what Miye does best. She takes the most ordinary settings and ideas and infuses them with a touch of magic. She did it with her *DallerGut Dream Department Store* duology, and she's done it again here – only this time, instead of whisking us away into a world of dreams, she drops us into a reality that feels, frankly, a little too real. For anyone navigating the day-to-day grind of salaried life, it hits close to home.

In fact, many Koreans begin their careers in some kind of office setting – it's a rite of passage and a near-universal backdrop to adult life. With its unspoken rules, quiet tensions, and repetitive rhythms, office life might seem mundane on the surface. But in Miye's hands, even that monotony becomes a stage for quiet drama, sharp satire, and unexpected emotional catharsis.

One of the most fascinating challenges in translating this story was capturing the voice of the narrator, Ice Cube. His tone hovers between socially awkward, obsessively detailed, and at times teetering on incel-adjacent. The goal was to preserve that uneasy edge while still making him compelling – and sometimes even unexpectedly sympathetic. It was a delicate tonal balance to strike, so that the twist at the end would pay off all the more effectively.

So yes, it all begins with something as mundane as a break room. But somewhere between the coffee mix hoarding, the unwashed tumblers, and the whispered office gossip, Miye uncovers something far more unsettling: the invisible fault lines that run between people. And in doing so, she leaves us with questions that linger – about perception, cancel culture, and how we treat those we barely know.

Read on for an excerpt from

DALLERGUT DREAM DEPARTMENT STORE

Prologue:

THE THIRD DISCIPLE'S HISTORIC STORE

Bobbed hair all soggy and puffy, wearing a comfortable shirt, Penny is sitting on the second floor of her favourite café. This morning, she received word from the DallerGut Dream Department Store that her application has passed the screening, and there will be an interview next week. She went straight to a corner bookstore to buy job interview books covering everything from guidelines to prep questions, and now she is in full prep mode.

But something has been bothering her for a while. A guy drinking his tea at the next table has been tapping his feet, showing off his colourful fuzzy socks with every bounce, distracting her like crazy.

He is in a thick dressing gown, sipping his tea with closed eyes. Its fresh forest scent carries over to her table whenever he blows on the tea. He must be having a special herbal tea, good for fatigue.

'Hmm, very nice . . . warm . . . how much . . . refill?' The guy mutters under his breath as though he is sleep-talking, then goes back to tapping his feet, smacking his lips.

Penny moves her seat to block his socks from view. Many

others in the café are wearing pyjamas. Sitting next to the staircase leading to the first floor is a lady in a rented dressing gown,
scratching the back of her neck and occasionally squirming as if
she is feeling uncomfortable.

For centuries, Penny's hometown has been famous for its
local sleep products, which have driven its growth, and now it
has evolved into a metropolis with a surging population. The
locals, including Penny, who grew up here, are used to seeing
outsiders roaming around in sleepwear.

Penny sips on her now-cold coffee. The awfully bitter caf-
feine goes down her throat, and it instantly seems to mute the
distracting background noise and calm the air surrounding her
body. The extra charge for two Calm Syrup pumps is worth it.
She pulls a prep question sheet toward her and re-reads the last
question, which she has been struggling with.

Q. Which dream and dreammaker won the Grand Prix at
   the 1999 Dream of the Year Awards by a unanimous vote?
   a. 'Crossing the Pacific Ocean as a Killer Whale' by
      Kick Slumber
   b. 'Living as My Parents for a Week' by Yasnoozz
      Otra
   c. 'Floating in Space Gazing Down on Earth' by
      Wawa Sleepland
   d. 'Teatime with a Historical Figure' by Doje
   e. 'An Infertile Couple's Dream Foretelling the Birth
      of Triplets' by Babynap Rockabye

Penny tries to work out the answer, chewing on her pen cap. It's tricky: 1999 was a long time ago. Young dream directors like Kick Slumber or Wawa Sleepland might not be correct. She strikes out the two choices with her pen. When did Yasnoozz Otra's 'Living as My Parents for a Week' come out? If Penny's memory serves her right, it was fairly recent. Otra's dreams usually get huge promotions before the release, and one of the catchphrases from their ads is still vivid in her memory – their model saying vivaciously, 'Still bothering to scold your kids? Make them live like you for a week in a dream, and everything is solved!'

Penny wavers between the two remaining options and finally goes with 'e', Babynap Rockabye's 'An Infertile Couple's Dream Foretelling the Birth of Triplets'. She is reaching for her coffee to take another sip when, out of nowhere, a furry paw slaps down on her question sheet, catching her so off guard that she almost knocks over her mug.

'No, the answer is "a",' says the owner of the big paw without an introduction. 'Kick Slumber debuted in 1999, and it was historic because he won the Grand Prix in his first year. I saved up money for six months straight to buy his dream. It was the most vivid dream I've had in my entire life! The feeling of my fins crossing the ocean and the view under the waves. It was so real that when I woke up, I was mortified that I hadn't been born a killer whale! He is a genius. You know how old he was then? Just thirteen!' The owner of the paw seems to burst with pride as if he were talking about his own accomplishment.

'Oh, it's you, Assam. You scared me.' Penny pushes away the mug out of harm's way. 'How did you know I was here?'

'I saw you coming out of the bookstore with a bunch of books. I knew you would hang around here. You never study at home.' Assam glances at the pile of books on Penny's table. 'Prepping for *the* job interview?'

'And how did you know that? I just heard from them this morning.'

'Nothing in this area goes unnoticed by us Noctilucas.'

Assam is one of the Noctilucas working on this street. Their job is to make sure the sleeping customers don't go around taking off their pyjamas. They chase after any naked customers, carrying a hundred dressing gowns on their shoulders. Their oversized paws, their claws, which are long enough to hang on to several dressing gowns at once, and their warm, furry bodies all make the job a good fit for them. The irony is that they don't wear anything either, but on second thought, Penny thinks the naked customers would feel more comfortable being chased by equally naked furry creatures than by well-dressed humans.

'You don't mind me sitting here, do you? My feet hurt from bustling around all day.' Assam plops down in the seat before Penny can answer. His fluffy tail sticks out through a hole in the back of the chair, wagging.

'This is hard.' Penny looks at the question again. 'How old are you if you know all this, Assam?'

'That is a rude question to ask a Noctiluca,' Assam says primly. 'I once studied hard to get into those stores too, but I quit. I thought this job suited me better.' He brushes down the gowns on his shoulder. 'Anyhow, I can't believe this is really happening. Clumsy Penny, getting an interview at the DallerGut Dream Department Store!'

'I guess my good karma finally comes into play!' Penny genuinely believes it is a miracle that she has passed the screening.

Working at the DallerGut Dream Department Store is a job coveted by every young person. The high pay, the glamorous architecture that is a city landmark, the various incentives and the thoughtful employee benefits of free dreams doled out on special occasions – there are just too many reasons to want to work there. The locals are familiar with the long pedigree of the DallerGut family. In fact, the family *is* the origin of the city. The prospect of working with Mr DallerGut makes Penny's heart swell so much that she thinks her whole body might swell up too, like a balloon.

'I really hope I get in,' Penny says, clasping her hands together as if in prayer.

'And you're studying just these books?' Assam holds up one of the prep books and skims through it before putting it back on the table.

'Thought I should memorise whatever I can. You never know what they'll ask. It could be naming the Legendary Big Five, or the highest-selling dream of the decade, or what time of day is popular among what customer demographic – who knows? I learned that the shift I applied for has a lot of West Australian and Asian customers. I even memorised all the time zones and datelines. Fun fact: do you know why our city has a constant influx of customers twenty-four seven?'

Penny is eager to launch into a long lecture right there and then, but Assam is also eager to avoid it, vigorously shaking his head. 'DallerGut would never ask such a boring question. Plus, any middle-schooler on the street would know the answer.'

When Penny turns glum, Assam holds out his paw to pat her on the shoulder. 'Don't worry, buddy. I've heard a lot about DallerGut after a decade of working here.' He is quick to continue before Penny can ask him his age again. 'And I hear he loves to ask ambiguous things about dreams, so I don't think his questions will have a clear answer. Speaking of which, I actually came here to give you this.' He drops the heap of dressing gowns from his shoulder on to the floor and starts rummaging through them. From among the mountain of gowns, he produces a small bundle. He unpacks it, and out come dozens of fuzzy socks.

'Wait, no, these are for the customers who have cold feet . . . Ah, yes, there it is!' Assam pulls a small book from the bundle. It has a hard, pale blue cover, and the elegant gold titling reads *The Time God and the Three Disciples.*

'I haven't seen that book in ages!' Penny recognises it at once. In fact, everyone else should know it if they grew up here. It is a popular book that is on the children's must-read list.

'DallerGut could ask about this story, you know. If you haven't read it since you were little, you should read it again – carefully, this time around. This is one of the most important stories of DallerGut, after all!' Assam pulls his seat closer toward

Penny, his face right next to hers. 'And just between us, I hear DallerGut gave this book to all the employees at the Dream Department Store.'

'Is that for real?' Penny asks, taking the book from Assam in a hurry.

'Of course! That proves how important he thinks this boo—' Assam stops abruptly as his eyes move from Penny to the view outside the window. 'Oh goodness! I should get back. I think I just saw a person roaming around in underwear.' His chestnut nose twitches. He rushes to pick up the pile of gowns while Penny helps to put the fuzzy socks back in the bundle.

'Good luck, Penny. Let me know how the interview goes.' Assam stands up, but his eyes are still preoccupied with the view outside. 'At least *that* guy is wearing something,' he mumbles.

'Thanks, Assam,' Penny says.

Assam's tail circles clockwise as if to say, 'You're welcome,' and off he goes downstairs.

Penny touches the book Assam left. He does have a point. Why hasn't she thought about re-reading this book? It explains the origin of this big shopping street, the birth of the city, and most of all, the genesis of the DallerGut Dream Department Store. If DallerGut values history, there is a good chance that the answers to his interview questions will be in this book. Penny tucks the sheets of practice questions inside her backpack. She finishes her remaining coffee in one go and straightens her back, then flips the book.

The Time God and the Three Disciples

Eons ago, there lived the Time God, who governed people's times. One day during their usual relaxed luncheon, the Time God realised there was little time left to live. The Time God summoned three disciples and shared the news.

The First Disciple, gallant and daring, asked their teacher what they should do next. The vulnerable Second Disciple brimmed with tears, lost in the memories they shared with the Time God. The last Third Disciple stood there without a word, waiting for the Time God to continue.

'My dearest Third Disciple, always considerate and cautious, let me ask you a question. If I divide time into three shards for each of you to govern, which shall you take – the past, the present or the future?' the Time God asked.

The Third Disciple pondered and said they would choose whatever was left after the First and Second Disciples had chosen.

The gallant and daring First Disciple did not let the opportunity pass, and said they would take the future. 'Please grant me power not to dwell on the past so I can govern the future,' they added.

The First Disciple always thought a timely grasp on the future without looking back was the most beautiful virtue. So, the Time God granted them the future, with the power to forget the past.

The Second Disciple cautiously requested that they take the past. They said holding on to the memories would make them forever happy without remorse or emptiness. So, the Time God granted them the past, with the power to forever cherish all old memories.

Now, holding the shard of the present – so small and sharp compared to the future and past – the Time God asked the Third Disciple, 'Shall you govern the momentary present?'

'No, teacher, please distribute it to all people equally,' the Third Disciple said.

The Time God was confused. 'Throughout all my years of teaching, there was no particular time that you considered special?' the Time God asked in disappointment.

This forced the Third Disciple to be candid. 'The time I love most is when everyone is asleep, teacher. That is when we do not dwell on regrets about the past or anxiety over the future. But people do not consider sleep in the happy memories they cherish or the grand futures they look forward to. Even people asleep in the present do not recognise they are asleep. How dare I, a measly being, come forward and say I shall govern this piteous time?'

The First Disciple secretly scoffed at them, while the Second Disciple was mildly surprised. They both thought sleep was a waste of time. But the Time God generously offered sleep time to the Third Disciple.

'Dear First and Second Disciples, do you mind if I take slices from your shards, past sleep and future sleep, and give them to the Third Disciple?' the Time God asked, and the

First and Second Disciples answered without hesitation, 'Not at all, teacher.'

So, the three disciples took their portion of time shards and dispersed. The First and Second Disciples, who each received the future and past, were very satisfied with the powers given to them by the Time God.

The First Disciple and their followers let go of all the tedious things from the past and were soon excited to build a grand new future, venturing out to a land much bigger than their own. Equally excited were the Second Disciple and their followers, who cherished the past, remembering their young, fair-skinned faces and loving memories.

But problems soon arose. The First Disciple was so occupied with the future that the sheer amount of the past they had entirely forgotten grew like a thick layer of fog in their land. They could no longer recognise their friends and family through the dense layers of haze. As memories with their beloved kinfolks were gone, so were their very reasons for aspiring to the future, which they could no longer remember. They became oblivious to what lay right before them, and even more so the far future.

The Second Disciple and their followers were no different. They were trapped in only the good memories, so they could not accept the passage of time, the inevitable partings and deaths. The tears of their weak souls constantly flowed down to the earth, creating a large cave in which they eventually hid, burying themselves deep inside.

Having witnessed all this, the Time God waited until everyone was sound asleep. Then, lit by the moonlight, the Time God snuck into their bedrooms. The Time God pulled out a sharp shard of the present and gripped it hard before using it to slice off their shadows. Holding the shadows in one hand and an empty bottle in the other, the Time God left in the darkness.

First, the Time God put the foggy memories the First Disciple and their followers had abandoned in the bottle. Then, the Time God fetched in their arms all the tears the Second Disciple and their followers had shed. Lastly, the Time God went to the Third Disciple in secret.

'To what do I owe the pleasure of this unannounced visit at night, teacher?' the Third Disciple asked.

Without a word, the Time God pulled them out one by one and placed them on the table – the sleeping shadows, the bottle of forgotten memories and the teardrops. The Third Disciple could not fathom the teacher's mind.

'How shall I help people with them?' the Third Disciple asked, but instead of an answer, the Time God picked up the shadows, saggy in deep sleep, and put them inside the bottle. The Time God added the teardrops to the bottle as the shadows struggled to open their eyes.

Then a wonder occurred. The tears gathered to become the eyes of the shadows. The eyes opened wide, the shadows coming to life inside the bottle of memories.

'Let the shadow of people be awake when they are asleep,'

said the Time God as they handed the bottle of shadows and memories to the Third Disciple.

As wise as the Third Disciple was, they had no idea what their teacher meant. 'Do you mean to let people think and feel, even in their sleep? How would that be any help for them?'

'All the memories the shadows will experience during sleep will strengthen weak souls, unlike the Second Disciple. And when they wake up the next day, they will be reminded of the important things and not forget, unlike the careless First Disciple.'

After the Time God had delivered this speech, the Third Disciple realised their time for the lesson was ending. The Third Disciple shouted in haste as their teacher faded little by little. 'Please enlighten me further, teacher. How can I teach people to understand all this? I cannot even begin to define what *this* is.'

The Time God smiled and said, 'You do not need to understand. It is better that you do not. Time will come when people start to embrace it.'

'Could you at least give this a name? Shall I call it a miracle? Or an illusion?' the Third Disciple asked desperately.

'Call it a dream. You will make them dream every night.' And with that, the Time God vanished without a trace.

Penny closes the book, odd sensations stirring inside her. The story had seemed distant and outrageous when she first read it as a child. A fairy tale. But how many things in the world can you understand without believing in them? Everyone in the city accepts the story as naturally as one accepts the circle of life – from nonexistence to birth, and from futile existence to death. The very existence of people dreaming every night and the Third Disciple later founding the Dream Department Store, which was then inherited by their descendants and now passed down to DallerGut – all of this is living proof.

Suddenly, DallerGut seems like a mythical figure to Penny. The thought of having a conversation with him one-on-one leaves her half excited and half nervous. She slightly shudders, a chill in her belly. *I guess I'm done for today*, she thinks.

Penny returns home with the pile of books in her backpack, and for the rest of the day, until she falls asleep, she doesn't put down the book that Assam gave her. She reads and re-reads it for several days until D-day. She reads it so many times that she has memorised the entire story.

On the day of the interview, Penny arrives at the department store early, looking for DallerGut's office in the lobby on the first floor. People wear stretched T-shirts and loose shorts as pyjamas, or dressing gowns provided by the Noctilucas. They are all looking at different dream products in the display corner. Next to the 'Best New Products' stand, a customer in pyjama bottoms covered with stars is holding a dream box. 'Oh, the new dream by Kick Slumber is here . . . "Becoming a Giant Tortoise in Galapagos". Let's see. These snobby critics rated it four point nine? That's new. But what is this? "A spectacular

abyss surrounding its carapace"? Their blurbs are useless as usual.'
Penny has ten minutes to get to DallerGut's office, but there is
nowhere here that looks fancy enough to be the owner's office.

Penny intends to ask a middle-aged employee at the front
desk, but she is on the phone and seems too busy. Same with the
other employees who are moving past in linen aprons, barely
noticing Penny.

'Mum! I flunked it!' yells a passer-by on the phone, bumping
into Penny. 'He asked the craziest questions ever. I'd analysed
the last five years of dream trends, but he didn't ask anything
about that!'

She must have had an interview with DallerGut! Desperately,
Penny tries to ask her in big airy mouth movements, 'Where.
Is. The. Office?'

The woman bluntly points up the stairs before rushing away
through the crowd. The wooden staircase leads up to the next
floor. Looking more closely, Penny sees a half-open wooden
door with a dangling sign that reads 'Interview Room'. The
peeled-off paint on the door and the rough handwriting on the
paper make it look like the entrance to an old-school classroom.

In front of the door, Penny takes a moment to breathe and
calm herself. Then, still unsure if this is DallerGut's office, she
knocks on the door as a courtesy.

'Yes, do come in.' A booming voice rings from the inside.
The same voice Penny has often heard in TV interviews or radio
broadcasts. There is no doubt that DallerGut is inside the room.

'Excuse me.'

The office is smaller than it looks from the outside. DallerGut is struggling with an old printer behind a long desk. 'Welcome. Do you mind giving me a second? I have issues every time I print with this thing.'

He is wearing a clean shirt, and looks way taller and skinnier than he does on TV or in magazines. His dishevelled, wavy hair shows streaks of grey. DallerGut forcibly pulls out what looks like Penny's resume from the printer. Having been jammed somewhere inside the machine, the paper is all crumpled with the end cut off, but he seems satisfied. 'Finally.'

Penny walks closer to DallerGut as he offers his wrinkled, skinny hand. Penny, feeling nervous, quickly rubs her hand against her clothes before shaking his. 'Hello, Mr DallerGut, I am Penny.'

'Nice to meet you, Penny. I was looking forward to meeting you.' DallerGut looks regal. On closer inspection, his dark brown eyes exude youthful twinkles, more like the eyes of a boy. Penny feels she has stared at him too intently and looks away at the boxes strewn all over the office, which looks more like a shabby warehouse. All dream products. Some are damp from long days spent here, and some seem new with their wrapping still shiny. DallerGut pulls a steel chair closer, drawing her attention back to him.

'Please have a seat.' He points to a nearby chair. 'Make yourself comfortable. These are my favourite cookies. Here, have some.' DallerGut hands Penny a savoury-looking nutty cookie.

'Thank you,' Penny says, and as she takes a bite, the air turns cooler, and her shoulders relax. Strangely, the once mysterious office becomes more familiar. She feels like she did when she had the Calm Syrup added to her coffee, only much better this time. There must be something more to his cookie.

'I remember your name very clearly,' DallerGut says. 'Your application was impressive. I particularly love that phrase of yours: "As much as you love them, dreams are just dreams."'

'I'm sorry? Oh, that . . . That was . . .' She now remembers having put the phrase in her otherwise-too-bland application, just to stand out from the rest and pique DallerGut's interest. *Did he just want to figure out who this daring kid was?*

Penny quickly gauges DallerGut's expression. Fortunately, there is no look of, *Let me see how this kid reacts.* He seems genuinely interested in her.

'It is great to hear that I made an impression, sir,' Penny carefully responds.

'Shall we get down to business, then?' DallerGut looks toward the ceiling, thinking of his questions. 'First, I would like to hear your honest opinion about dreams, Penny.'

He has started with a tricky one. Penny takes a deep breath and tries to remember the model answer she saw in the job interview prep books.

'So . . . Dreams let us experience things we otherwise couldn't in reality . . . They serve as a substitute to the unrealistic possibilities . . .' Penny notices DallerGut's disappointed look and suspects that many interviewees who came before her would probably have answered in the same way.

'That does not sound like the person who wrote this application.' DallerGut doesn't look Penny in the eye as he touches the
corner of the document. Penny's gut tells her that her response
has just called upon the shadow of impending rejection looming
over her. She needs to turn the tide.

'But even if we can experience the unrealistic in dreams, they
can never be real!' Penny has no idea what she is talking about.
All she wants is to stand out from the rest of the applicants. She
has a strong feeling this is what DallerGut is looking for above
all. Also, if the daring statement of 'Dreams are just dreams' on
her application got her past the screening stage, she might as
well stick to this path.

'No matter how good a dream you have, when you wake
up, that is it.'

'Why so?' DallerGut looks rather serious.

Penny is baffled. Of course, there is no plausible reasoning
behind her impromptu response. She knows it is rude, but she
stuffs down the rest of the cookie to get some soothing help.
'No particular reason, sir. I just heard that customers sometimes
forget about their dreams afterwards. I literally meant that
dreams are just dreams, because they are gone once you wake
up. And that is why they do not interfere with reality. I like that
part of not overstepping the line.'

Penny swallows hard. She was rambling out of fear of pro-
longed silence, which she worried might ruin the interview.
But now it becomes apparent that it is her answer that has just
killed the mood.

'I see. Is that all?' DallerGut asks indifferently.

Now that she has ruined it anyway, Penny decides to at least show all that she has prepared for the interview. This seems to be her only chance before she is dismissed.

'I have read *The Time God and the Three Disciples* many times. In the story, the Third Disciple rules the "sleep time", which the other disciples did not care about.'

DallerGut's look confirms that reading the book after Assam's suggestion was a perfect choice. The attention and interest he had shown her earlier returned.

'I didn't understand the Third Disciple's choice,' Penny continues. 'The First Disciple chooses the future, which has infinite possibilities. And the Second Disciple chooses the past, with all its precious experiences. Hopes for the future and lessons from the past. These two are very important things for living in the present.'

DallerGut nods subtly. Penny doesn't stop.

'But what about when you are asleep? Nothing happens. We just lie down for hours. It is a rest in name only, and some people even think it's a waste of time. Because if you think about it, dozens of years of your life are spent just lying down! But the Time God leaves this sleep time to their most beloved Third Disciple and asks them to make people dream during sleep. Why is that?' Penny lets the question hang in the air for a moment, buying herself some time. 'Whenever I think of dreams, I ask myself this question: why do people sleep and dream? I think it is because everyone is insecure and foolish in their own way.

Some are like the First Disciple and always look ahead, and some linger in the past like the Second Disciple. But for all of us, it is easy to forget important things. I think the Time God assigns sleep time to the Third Disciple to help people. You know how yesterday's worries are gone after a good night's sleep, and we are fully refreshed to start a new day? That's it! Whether you have a good dream you bought from this department store or do not dream at all, all of us sleep in one way or another to get closure from yesterday and prepare for tomorrow. In that sense, sleep is no longer a waste of time.'

Penny has managed to come up with a decent answer, pulling it together from what she read in the book. She is surprised by how exceptionally articulate she has been today. *Reading books does go a long way, as they say.* Now feeling more confident, she wants to end on a high note by adding just a touch more bedazzle.

'So I think sleep and dreams are . . . like a comma God meticulously designed in the middle of a breathless straight line called life!' Penny finishes, feeling proud of herself. DallerGut looks inscrutable. Penny tightens her lips as she realises her last sentence was perhaps too on the nose. She should have stopped when things were going great.

Silence hangs in the air. Quiet and calm, it almost feels like a separate world from beyond the door, where crowds of customers are still shopping. Penny suddenly feels parched with thirst. DallerGut scribbles something on her resume.

'Thank you for your insight. You seem to have given a lot of thought to dreams.' DallerGut clasps his hands and looks straight into her eyes. 'Let me end with my last question. As you know, there are many other dream stores besides ours. Please tell me if there are any particular reasons you want to join us.'

Penny almost wants to mention the high pay but decides not to, figuring it would be too blunt for a first impression. She carefully chooses her words and responds slowly. 'Many dream stores are springing up everywhere and selling provocative dreams. I remember something you said in the magazine, *Interpretations Better Than Dreams*. You mentioned that some stores lure people in by offering more sleep than they really need and for pleasure only. And I heard that your store is different. You only offer dreams that people need and always emphasise that reality is important. I think these were the boundaries the Time God wanted the Third Disciple to govern. Just the right amount of control without overstepping the realm of reality. That's why I applied here.'

DallerGut finally gives a wide smile, which Penny thinks makes him look a decade younger. His dark brown eyes gaze steadily at her.

'Penny, can you start tomorrow?'

'Of course!' The once-muted background noises start seeping into the office room. The moment Penny gets her first job.

I.

THE DALLERGUT DEPARTMENT STORE RUSH HOUR

It is Penny's first day of work, and she is already running late, gasping and panting, with beads of sweat on the bridge of her nose. She had a celebratory dinner with her family yesterday before chatting the night away with her friends, hence the oversleeping. The call with Assam went on for an especially long time as he was very keen to know every detail about how helpful his book had been.

'So when you said that, how did his face change again? Oh, my goodness, that book was indeed the silver bullet! You know, the book *I* gave, right?'

Penny promised to treat him well, finally making him hang up the phone.

Today, the city is especially swarming with locals and sleep customers. Penny quickly pushes through the crowd, frequently bumping into their shoulders and apologising. She finally catches her breath when she arrives at the back alley of the DallerGut Department Store. It looks like she can make it on time.

The alley is filled with the savoury scents of roasted fruits and boiling milk. Having not eaten today, Penny looks around to see if she can pick up a fruit skewer on the go, but the line is too long.

'What's up with today? So many people,' says one of the food-truck cooks, overwhelmed. He is flipping over fruit skewers on the grill using one hand and whipping a massive pot with a ladle with his other hand. Caramelised onion milk is boiling inside the pot. It is a popular recipe known for helping people fall into a deep sleep.

Several customers are already sipping onion milk from their mugs in front of the food truck. Some older people look relaxed and satisfied, while some kids have a sip and immediately scowl. One kid deliberately spills milk on the floor.

'No waste on the floor, please!' A Noctiluca appears out of nowhere, shaking his furry paws as he steps in between the kids and Penny. A lot smaller than Assam, he starts wiping the milk from the floor, grumbling. Penny quickly moves away so as not to get any milk on her socks. She is not wearing shoes today, as she wanted to run fast and comfortably.

It is not uncommon to walk without shoes here. The street has a strict sanitary policy to ensure it is as clean as indoor floors because sleeping customers rarely wear shoes. Naturally, the locals have also taken to walking in socks for a quick stroll.

But this has caused an unexpected crisis for the Leprechauns, who have been artisan shoemakers for generations. People now shop more for socks and less for shoes, which has led to less business in their shoe store. The Leprechauns have since ventured out to expand their business areas by boldly tapping into the dream-production industry too. Assam told Penny that their revenues soared by 1,000% after their business expansion. That sounds believable, given that the Leprechauns' shoe store has just moved from the cheap corner spot to a bigger space in the main street.

As she passes, Penny glances at the Leprechauns' store window display, located right next to the DallerGut Dream Department Store. It has a big sign and lots of other product posters here and there, making it hard to see the inside of the store.

Looking for Winged Shoes, Lightspeed Skate Shoes, and Special Flippers for Graceful Swimming? Come inside! Interested in a Flying Dream, Sprinting Dream, or Swimming Dream that harnesses the essence of the Leprechauns' master technology? Visit us in the DallerGut Dream Department Store next door, on the third floor!

'Papa, can I have winged shoes?' a girl asks her dad.

'Those shoes can break quickly, sweetie. The best shoes do not need additional functions, just strong soles.'

'Wah-wah! I won't go if you don't buy me the shoes.' She flops down, throwing a temper tantrum.

Penny passes the father and daughter and finally arrives at the Dream Department Store. She pulls out a pair of loafers from her purse and does a last-minute check on her face with a palm-sized mirror. Her bobbed hair looks especially poised today. With her tiny nose and big, gentle eyes, her first impression doesn't seem too bad. The only downside is the wrinkled blouse she forgot to iron, but she can do nothing about it now.

As she steps inside the department store, she is instantly enmeshed in the enormous throng of customers. At the lobby's front desk, an employee is making announcements with a microphone. It is the same middle-aged woman Penny saw yesterday, who was busy on the phone.

'Attention to the outsiders only. All costs are deferred payments! You may leave once you receive your dream! Hey, Dojicom siblings! That doesn't apply to you. You guys come and pay first!' A young, freckled brother and sister get caught trying to sneak through the back door. They trudge toward the front desk.

Penny is confused about whether she should go to DallerGut's office first or just change into the employee uniform, an apron. Dilly-dallying between the crowds, she is instantly grabbed by the hem and pushed behind the front desk by someone.

'You're new today, right? Nice to meet you. Now keep on your toes. We have a busy day today.' The middle-aged woman who was just giving announcements smiles at Penny. 'My name is Weather,' she continues. 'I am the manager of the first floor. But these titles are useless, so just call me Weather. I have a daughter around your age and a baby boy. Been working here for thirty years. Should be enough for my introduction!'

She seems genuinely bright and cool, except she looks

exhausted today. Her red curly hair is drooping feebly, and her voice has gone raspy.

'Hello, Weather. I'm Penny. Yes, today is my first day here. And so . . . What should I do first?'

'DallerGut asked me to give you a guide to the store. As you know, each of our five floors sells different genres of dreams. You don't need to worry about the first floor – DallerGut and myself, with other veteran employees, handle the customers here. From the second to the fifth floor, you will go upstairs and meet each floor manager. They will explain their floors to you. Then, you will tell us which floor you want to work on. But if none of the managers like you, well, you may have to go home . . .'

Penny is all wound up, blinking her large eyes in shock.

'I was just joking.' Weather shakes her hand. She looks hot, and as she takes off her jacket, her shirt is drenched with sweat, even with the air conditioning. 'Now, off you go. I must get back to work. So many people today.'

Penny heads out from the front desk. Weather quickly disappears out of sight, hidden by a flock of customers pushing toward the front desk. But Penny can hear her yelling, 'How about "The Reunion with an Old Friend" product? There is only one left in stock on the second floor! Were you asking what kind of old friend it would be? I have no idea! Possibly one of your childhood friends that you still remember?'

'"Three Nights in the Maldives" was out of stock as soon as they came in.'

'I'm sorry, but this dream is already reserved. No ripping

the package!'

'Chuck Dale's "Five Senses of Sensual Dream Series" was just taken a minute ago by a group of teenage customers.'

'All floors will be sold out soon. ALL SOLD OUT SOON!'

Away from Weather's desperate calls, Penny turns toward the elevator. There is already a long line of people waiting, so she decides to take the staircase next to DallerGut's office. She wonders if she should stop by and say hello, but decides to return later after seeing a handwritten sign that reads 'Temporarily Away'. DallerGut's printer must still be broken. The wooden staircases are so steep that by the time Penny reaches the second floor, her thighs already feel numb. At least she won't need any additional workouts if she uses these staircases for work.

At first glance, the second floor looks clean, without a speck of dust. With a simple wooden interior style and evenly placed lighting fixtures, even the product tags look as consistent as clockwork. Most of the display stands are empty, but the few items still in stock are placed at exactly the same angle, each with the same ribbon tied to them. The employees in their aprons walk around the display stands, extremely conscientious and anxious as they look after the customers, who are examining products and then putting them back in a disorderly fashion.

While the first floor sells only a handful of high-end, popular or limited-edition, pre-ordered products, the second floor sells more generic dreams. Also known as 'The Daily' corner, the second floor displays dreams of simplicity, like going on quick getaways, hanging out with friends, and enjoying good food.

In front of the staircase where Penny stands is a display stand marked 'Memories'. Inside it is a luxurious leather case labelled: 'No Refund Once Unsealed'. Only a few dreams remain inside.

'What is this dream about?' After looking around at the products, a woman calls for an employee.

'It's about childhood memories, where one of your favourite memories will replay in your dream! The stories may be different depending on the dreamer. In my case, I had a dream where I lay on my mother's lap while she cleaned my ears. Her scent and the languid atmosphere — it was all so real. It was wonderful.' The employee stares into space, daydreaming.

'I'll have it, then. Can I buy several of them?'

'Of course. Many of our customers buy two or three a night.'

Penny tiptoes to look around the entire second floor. A middle-aged man who seems to be the floor manager is talking to a customer in a corner that has been decorated as a modern bedroom. Penny carefully approaches him so as not to interrupt their conversation.

His look really does scream 'Manager'. While all other employees wear aprons around their waists bearing a brooch carved with the number '2', he flaunts a lavish jacket, the brooch on his left lapel. He seems wiry and shrewd.

'Why can't I buy it?' asks a young male customer, confused.

'I'm sorry, but how about you come by another time? I'm afraid too many thoughts are distracting you right now, and they'll obscure the clarity of the dream. It's better to have a good night's sleep first. I've seen ninety-nine per cent of customers like yourself have their thoughts creep in and change their dreams to an entirely different story. There's some amazing onion milk on the next street. It helps you sleep well. I'd recommend that you try it and get some sleep first.'

The customer grumbles and goes off toward the elevator. The manager-looking man picks up the product the customer has left behind, wipes it with his handkerchief, and places it back on the shelf, carefully straightening the angle.

'Excuse me . . . Are you the manager for the second floor?' Penny asks politely and cautiously. The man is wearing pristinely ironed trousers, and his shoes do not have even a speck of dust. His moustache is neatly trimmed. His hair, too short for grooming, is pulled back with oily wax. Penny finds him difficult to approach.

'Yes, I am. Vigo Myers is my name. First day of work here?'

'Er, yes. I'm Penny. How did you know?' Penny covers her cheeks to hide any indication of 'amateur' or 'newbie' on her face.

'Customers rarely come to me first. They usually call for other employees. They say I'm not easy to talk to, which I don't mind. So that gave you away, and you didn't look familiar. It was a natural deduction.' Myers folds his arms and gives Penny a stern look. 'You must be on a floor tour. I remember the boss mentioning you.'

'Yes, that's right.'

'Good. Any questions about my floor?'

Penny's biggest question is how they can tie the ribbon decorations into such a perfect bow for every single product, but she holds back and asks her second-biggest question instead.

'Why didn't you sell the dream to that customer?'

'Good question.' Myers loosens his arms and strokes one of the display stands. 'All the dreams on this floor are some of the best products that I've curated through meticulous inspection. The last thing I want to see is the customers returning to complain about how silly the dreams are. Remember – you shouldn't sell dreams to just anybody, or you won't get the payment they deserve.'

Penny knows the store takes deferred payments from outside customers, but that's all she knows. She nods, pretending she understands.

'Newbies these days. I heard all they do is bring a cover letter and have a quick interview with DallerGut. And just like that, they're in!' Myers scoffs in sotto voce.

'Yes . . . I mean, that's how I got in, too.'

'Well, that's preposterous! I'm thinking of requiring another round of tests for the employees on my floor. The uncertainty and discontinuity of dreams, and their flexible and perilous nature, cannot be grasped with moderate knowledge. No, sir! Did you know I double-majored in Dreamatography and Dream Neuroscience? My thesis was published in more academic journals than I can count. My knowledge has been enormously helpful in my work here. Weather may have gotten her manager position on the first floor because she's worked with DallerGut longer, but I have earned my place purely by talent. You don't think I'm here by luck, do you?'

'Of course not. That is amazing!'

Penny doesn't want to be bothered with doing extra tests to work on the second floor. It seems that Myers realises this, as he steps back to shout at his employees. 'All right, everyone! All remaining items on the third display, go to the first! Let's move. Chop-chop!'

'Yes, manager!'

The employees swiftly go into motion at Myers' command. Their linen aprons are smooth as if freshly ironed, making Penny keenly aware of the wrinkled edges of her blouse, which she struggles to pull straight as she heads upstairs.

The third floor is merrier in comparison. The product posters patched across the wall come together surprisingly well, making a colourful, trendy wallpaper. A recent hit song plays through the speakers.

There is excitement among the dream buyers, not to mention the employees. One staffer is in full sales mode with a customer, intent on selling a fancy dream box with powder-pink, heart-shaped ornaments dangling from it.

'Chuck Dale's "Sensual Dream Series" is always out of stock. How about this one by Keith Gruer? If you're lucky enough, you might go on a dream date with your dream date in your dream!' At the slightest interest displayed by the customer, the employee adds, almost inaudibly, 'The caveat is that depending on your condition, the person you go on a date with can be completely random.'

The third-floor staff seem more carefree. They have each modified their work aprons to their own liking. One has hers turned into a princess-style dress, while another has a badge with a picture of his favourite dreammaker pinned to his apron. One staffer, busy replacing a small bulb inside a display case, has a huge pocket sewn on to her apron so that she can carry a stash of chocolate bars.

Penny's eyes are busy looking for someone who looks like a manager. No one seems to stand out by wearing a more senior uniform or looking more experienced. Penny approaches a nearby employee cleaning a display case, wearing a typical linen apron.

'Excuse me, can you direct me to the floor manager? Today is my first day and I'm on a tour.'

'Oh my god – a newbie! You're looking at her. Mogberry here. I'm the manager on the third floor.'

She is wearing the same uniform as the other employees. Her short, curly hair is tied back, but thin baby hairs stick out all over. Mogberry looks too young to be a manager, her rosy cheeks adding to her youthful looks.

Penny gives her a polite bow. 'My name is Penny. DallerGut instructed me to take a look around the store, so here I am.'

'So I've heard. Welcome to the third floor!' says Mogberry with a wide smile. 'This is where all the groundbreaking and fun activity dreams are. Oh, sorry, would you excuse me for a second?' Mogberry turns and asks a customer hovering nearby, 'Can I help you, ma'am? Any specific dream you're looking for?

If you have any preference, let me know. I can suggest some recommendations.'

The customer is wearing sporty shorts and a sleeveless top with a long neckline that stretches down to his chest. He looks like a middle-schooler. As if feeling cold, he constantly rubs his hands together.

'I'm looking for one where I'm the centre of attention. Better if the whole world revolves around me. The last dream I bought, I showed off a cool rap performance in front of the entire class at a school festival, and I felt like one of those dope kids.'

'There aren't many left in stock . . . Oh, how about this sci-fi movie series? Superhero movies are big these days. You can be a crimson iron hero or an invincible green monster. The dream-maker, Celine Gluck, is famous for her attention to detail, so you would be instantly immersed in the world.'

'Awesome. I actually saw a superhero movie today! So yes, I'll definitely have one, please!'

Mogberry smiles in satisfaction at striking the deal. The customer takes the product from her and tucks it under his arm as he disappears to the opposite side of the floor to browse the other dreams.

Penny watches him disappear. She suddenly remembers the notice she saw hanging in the Leprechauns' shoe store window on her way to work.

'I heard "Flying Dream" by the Leprechauns is on the third floor. Are those sold out already?' Penny asks.

Mogberry, who has been all smiles, suddenly frowns. 'Flying

dreams are always out of stock. Do you know how cunning these Leprechaun scoundrels are? I wouldn't say I liked it from the beginning when those shoe-making brats started getting into the dream business out of the blue. Sure enough, I caught them in their delivery sneaking in dreams that make you feel immobile, like your feet are made of steel! They say it's for good business, that you can get paid more this way. When I called them out on it, they threatened to cut supplies if I don't stay out of their business because, you know, only they can make those dreams. I mean, what nonsense is that?'

Penny regrets not having studied about the dream payment system. Why do those immobile dreams pay better? She cannot understand the logic. She has come across economics books like *The Economics of Deferred Dream Payments* and *Sell Dreams, Buy a House* at bookstores, but she has never dared to read them. She is hopeless with money or just anything number-related. Penny wants to ask Mogberry but decides not to, afraid to give off the impression of an underqualified novice that could jeopardise her chances of getting a job on any of the floors.

'DallerGut is too much of a softie. I think he should cut the deal with the Leprechauns!' the third-floor manager grumbles, growing more disgruntled the more she broods. With every word Mogberry sputters in her rage, more curly baby hairs spring out from the crown of her head like mini slinkies. It has now come to the point where she has more hair sticking out than in the ponytail.

Penny starts to peek around, looking for a way out to the

fourth floor as Mogberry's complaining drags on and on. Just then, Mogberry finds her next victim in another employee passing by, and begins venting to them about the Leprechauns instead, so Penny is able to escape the third floor.

Secretly, Penny has high hopes for the fourth floor. It sells nap-exclusive dreams, and she hears these are popular among animal customers, who tend to sleep lightly, or baby customers, who tend to sleep all day. Basically, she would be surrounded by adorable customers while working, and that alone is enough reason to build anticipation.

Penny steps on to the fourth floor in excitement. She spots a few adorable and tiny customers, but overall, it is not quite as she imagined it to be, as there are many adults and scary-looking animals here, too. The fourth floor has a lower ceiling compared to the other floors. The display stands only reach as far as her ankles. She feels like she is at a flea market where products are strewn over a large mat.

Sticking close to the wall, Penny tries to sidestep a sloth lying in the middle of the corridor and being poked by a giggling toddler. By Penny's feet, a display stand reads, 'Playing with Owner'. An old, furless dog sniffs around to carefully select a dream. Penny steps slightly aside so as not to disturb the canine customer.

'Knock, knock.' Someone taps on Penny's back, startling her. She turns around to find a man in a jumpsuit with long, dishevelled hair, staring at her.

'Hiya, you must be the newbie. Why didn't you come see me

first, dear?' he asks slyly.

'Oh, hello. I'm Penny. I got carried away, just looking around . . . Are you the manager of the fourth floor?'

'Sure am! I'm Speedo, and I'm the manager, indeed! Who else would the manager be?' Speedo is a fast talker. 'This floor is always busy. There's just so much demand. D'you know what the most important thing is on this floor?'

Penny feels somewhat lost, but Speedo seems determined to carry on, so she tries to look curious out of courtesy. Speedo haughtily raises his jaw to a forty-five-degree angle, running his left hand through his long hair. He has a sparse, less-than-ten-strand beard on his chin. Penny tries to avoid looking at his facial expression and focuses on the brooch on his chest instead. The silver brooch flashes the carved number '4'.

'Of course you don't know. Listen carefully. The key is to make sure these napping customers do not sleep too deeply from our dreams. Long naps make babies cry, and deep slumber makes animals easy prey. So, when in doubt, it's best not to sell our dreams at all. The sales will all be taken care of by other floors, anyway.'

Speedo doesn't stop showing off. He must have been dying to do so, with so few people around to boast to.

'Any questions for me?'

'Well . . .' Penny tries to come up with one, but Speedo doesn't allow her more than five seconds.

'You wanted to ask why I always wear this jumpsuit, didn't you? People always ask me that!'

Penny fails to hide her 'Well, no' expression, but fortunately,

Speedo doesn't care.

'I always think putting on the top and the bottoms separately is a waste of time. I would rather get more sleep in the morning. Oh, you must wonder – how do I go to the bathroom with this on? Clothes nowadays are so cleverly designed; you unzip it here—'

'Thanks, Speedo, but no need. I think I know.'

'You do? Then can you please get out of my way? It's about time the nappers from Spain start to swarm in here.' Speedo takes off as hastily as he has been talking. In an instant, he is already on to one of the customers and conversing. 'Oh, you have a good eye! The one you're looking at is called "Fatigue Recovery". Only two left in stock. There's no better nap dream than this! What do you think? Shall I get one for you or two?'

Startled, the customer puts down the product and trots off. Now more of them are leaving, overwhelmed by Speedo's aggressive customer service, but Speedo seems oblivious as he continues to sweep across the entire floor.

'Hey, Penny, you still here?' Speedo is next to Penny before she knows it, whispering into her ear out of the blue.

Penny hopes she won't be assigned to the fourth floor. She is feeling increasingly distraught. There is still the fifth floor, but the fifth floor only sells leftover dreams from the first, second, third and fourth floors. She lets go of any expectations that the fifth floor will have a better work environment.

The first thing she notices when she arrives on the fifth floor are banners hanging chaotically from everywhere. She pushes one of them aside, an old banner that reads: 'Blowout Sale on Expiring Products!'

The fifth floor is much more crowded than the other floors, filled with customers and employees. A slew of dream boxes on the central display stand looks like they have been dumped there all at once. Sticky notes and signs are sloppily plastered across the stand.

80% OFF SUPER SALE!

PLEASE NOTE: ALL DREAMS HERE ARE IN BLACK AND WHITE. IF YOU WISH TO PURCHASE COLOURED VERSIONS, PLEASE REACH OUT TO THE STAFF ON OTHER FLOORS.

Below the signs lie dream boxes with hashtags like: '#EatingAWholeLobsterAtAPrivateBeach' and '#SunsetInThe SouthernIslandShore'. Penny pictures a black-and-white scene – a black lobster and the sombre grey ocean – then shakes her head. *So this is what you call a "buy cheap, buy twice situation"*, she thinks.

'Dear customers, this is a real treasure hunt! Some dreams were originally priced at fifty gordens, and you can also find dreams made by the Legendary Big Five! Some were once limited editions! They are all hiding in here somewhere, waiting to be found! Keep your eyes peeled for your very own treasures!'

Penny looks at the back of the employee, who is gesturing exaggeratedly on top of the display stand opposite. Round shoulders, a chubby build, and comparatively nimble moves . . . His silhouette seems strangely familiar.

'Motail!'

'Penny! Had no idea *you* were the new hire!' Motail excitedly greets her in return. Penny's high-school friend and one of the loudest students, he always loved to be the centre of attention, and was also well known for doing incredible impersonations of the teachers.

'Are you the manager here . . .?'

'Of course not! Though I hope so one day. There is no manager on the fifth floor. We are free to sell dreams however we want, at our own discretion. Perfect for me!' As Motail talks, his body keeps bouncing around, and he continues selling dreams to the customers below him. 'Today's on me, guys! You can buy one and get one free! Out of my own salary!'

'Are you sure you'll be okay to make that decision yourself?' Penny asks worriedly.

'It's a lie. I was selling it at double the price in the first place.' Motail takes off his corduroy jacket and drapes it over his shoulders like a cape before he goes back to bouncing about here and there. This place does suit him perfectly. Penny pictures herself dancing around and selling dreams on the display stand like Motail, and it quickly makes her heart sink.

'Hey, Penny! Look at these. Some great products just came in!'

Before Penny knows it, Motail is already down from the display stand and next to her. In his hand is a dream box with a translucent blueish wrapper.

'Is this . . .?'

'Yes! It's by Wawa Sleepland. "A Week in Tibet!" The view

will be gorgeous. Of course, bits and pieces will be in black and white, but still. Sleepland creates scenery that's far more awesome than in real life. You know that, right?'

'But how come such a precious dream ended up here?' Penny is confused. Wawa Sleepland is one of the Legendary Big Five. Her dreams rarely become available, even with months of wait-listing.

'One of her customers ordered a made-to-order dream but failed to pick it up in time. I heard it was during midterms or something, so the customer apparently pulled an all-nighter. Any products not picked up in time also end up here on the fifth floor. I'm going to hide this until my shift ends, then I'll take it with me,' says Motail, smiling mischievously as he pushes the box deep inside the space below the display stand. 'Please don't say anything to DallerGut, Penny! I want to keep my job,' he adds, showing his snaggletooth grin. 'And also, give some thought to applying for the fifth floor. Here, you get incentives for your sales!'

Penny eyes grow wide.

Motail adds, 'But the base wage is way low.'

Now, Penny has to return to the first floor and meet DallerGut. Instead of taking the elevator, she takes the stairs to allow herself some time.

She starts weighing the risks of working on each floor. If she is to work on the fifth floor, she would have to train herself to sing in public, become reborn as a new person, or try every means possible to change her personality. The fourth floor would require her to tackle the task of working with Speedo. The third floor seems fun enough, except she'd need to be careful when picking a topic to talk about with Mogberry. And to work with Vigo Myers on the second floor, she would need to start ironing her blouse every day before she even tries to pass his test. Just as she passes the second floor, she hears Myers shouting, 'All products are sold out on the second floor! All sold out!'

Penny arrives on the first floor in front of DallerGut's office, still undecided about where she wants to work. The 'Temporarily Away' sign that was on the door earlier is now gone. She is about to knock on the door when she notices it's ajar. She peeks inside. DallerGut has company — it's Weather from the front desk.

'DallerGut, we are too old and worn out. We're long past the young days when a cheap lunch box was all we needed to recharge, and that was thirty years ago. We need more people at the front desk. It's too much work for us two to handle. Just look at us today. You were unavailable all day, taking care of the pre-orders in your office and keeping track of the inventory. I almost passed out covering for you,' Weather complains.

'I'm sorry, Weather. But you know how important the front desk job is. I can't entrust it to anyone. I'll try to post an opening internally to see if anyone within our staff is interested. Please bear with me a little longer. The work can get overwhelming, so I'm not quite sure if anyone is up for it . . . Oh yes! How about Vigo Myers from the second floor?'

'Myers?' Weather asks.

'With his experience and knowledge, he should be a great help,' DallerGut says gently.

'Oh, I don't think he would like the idea of working *for* me. Unless we offer him a managerial position for the first floor . . . Wait, who's there?' Weather seems to sense Penny's presence and turns toward the door.

Penny walks in, presenting an outward calm. 'I'm sorry, I didn't mean to interrupt. I just wanted to stop by and say I finished touring all the floors . . .'

'Oh, I see. It's fine! Please have a seat here.' DallerGut greets Penny with delight. He is wearing a soft cardigan, leaning back in his chair. 'So, which floor do you want to work on?' he asks.

'If I were you, I would choose the second floor. I can't say Vigo Myers is easy to work with, but you will learn a lot from him,' Weather adds. She also seems interested in hearing Penny's answer.

But Penny knows now that an appealing position has just opened up. And she does not want to let that opportunity slip away.

After a pause, she says in a firm voice, 'I want to work at the front desk.'

To her surprise, DallerGut and Weather accept her proposal without hesitation. Weather seems especially delighted that she will have support to take some of the load off her starting as early as today. And DallerGut, who must have been secretly afraid that Weather would drop a bomb and say 'I want to quit' or 'I decided to move to another store,' seems relieved that Penny has swooped in and saved him with the perfect solution.

The three walk out to the front desk so that Penny can be briefed on her new job. Behind the front desk are multiple security monitors following the state of each floor, and a microphone for making announcements. Brochures for customers are piled up on one side.

'Here, you can track each floor's inventory, sales and dream payment statuses,' Weather says, as she pulls up several complex windows on the computer monitor. 'This is Dream Pay Systems Version 4.5! It's the ultimate all-inclusive software with everything you need to run a store. The dream payment balance system it offers is especially top-notch. Comes with a steep cost, but it's all worth it. And if you want to use the automatic balance system that links to the safe . . . When the inventory falls below fourteen per cent, it will trigger an automatic warning . . .'

Penny realises she is drastically losing focus. She can barely follow every few words of Weather's speech. Surprisingly, DallerGut is wearing the same vacant look as Penny, standing there dumbfounded.

'I see you're another DallerGut, just as tech-averse. I'll tell you what the Eyelid Scale is.'

'Now *that's* something I can weigh in on!' DallerGut brightens.

Weather turns toward the wall, which circles the back of the front desk. On closer examination, the towering wall is a giant set of shelves with each level fully packed. On each shelf are small scales with numbers. The pendulums on the scales swing up and down like eyelids, indicating the sleep status. Located at around Penny's height sits a scale labelled 'No. 902', its marker quickly moving up and down between 'awake' and 'sleepy'.

'These are for our regulars. Specifically designed to predict their visiting hours. It is the product of our long-standing history of know-how,' DallerGut says with a proud look.

'This customer's eyelids always used to get droopy at around this hour,' Weather says, looking sentimentally at Eyelid Scale No. 999. 'But as the customer aged, he started sleeping way less. He rarely comes to buy dreams nowadays. You see, I share a lot of memories with them here. I gently stroke their eyelids sometimes, for customers who pre-order dreams and don't come to pick them up on time. But you should refrain from stroking them, really; you never know if they're in the middle of something important where they can't afford to doze off.'

Penny is so busy writing down notes that she barely has time to answer. 'Sorry, can you repeat what you just said? You do what to the eyelids?'

'It's fine. No worries – I will be working next to you anyway.'

The three are diving deeply into the Eyelid Scale conversation when an alarm pings by the front desk. It is coming from the 'Dream Pay Systems' monitor that Weather so highly praises.

'*Ding Dong. ALL PRODUCTS SOLD OUT. WE ARE CLEARED OF ALL STOCK!*'

'Work's done for today now that everything is sold out,' DallerGut says as he checks the notification and then announces through the microphone that everyone can leave work early.

There is roaring and cheering as soon as the announcement goes out.

'It's been ages since this happened! I should leave early, too. I have a family gathering tonight. My youngest can finally do a handstand! So we're going to celebrate,' Weather says.

All the employees, including Weather, leave one by one, and now, there are only DallerGut and Penny left. Penny also wants to leave, but she is waiting for her boss to go first, and he is still in the office. In the meantime, there are still customers snooping around the front gate.

'I'm sorry, all our products are sold out. We will open tomorrow as soon as we restock.'

Penny tries to feign her best apologetic look. Four or five customers in their sleepwear shrug and turn around to leave.

DallerGut, meanwhile, is scribbling something on a piece of paper at the front desk.

'What are you writing?' Penny asks.

'I'm writing a sold-out notice to hang on the front gate.'

Penny stands quietly, watching DallerGut. He has already thrown away three sheets of paper and is on the fourth draft because, apparently, he doesn't like his handwriting. Penny still finds it surreal that she is working with DallerGut. What is more, she is actually standing right next to him!

'Is the Third Disciple from the story really one of your ancestors?' Penny asks, out of the blue.

'That's what I'm told. My parents and grandparents always reminded me of that,' DallerGut responds nonchalantly as he picks bits of fluff from his cardigan.

'That's awesome!' Penny looks at DallerGut in complete awe.

'Done!' he exclaims, finally finishing off the sign.

'Here, let me put it up for you.' Penny takes out two long lines of tape and sticks up the notice nice and firmly. She stands back to check that it is straight before she comes back in.

All products are sold out today!

Thank you to our customers for visiting the DallerGut Dream Department Store on your way to sleep.

Please come back tomorrow! We are open all year round, twenty-four seven.

We will always have fantastic dream products waiting for you.

Yours truly,
DallerGut

'Time for some cookies!' DallerGut hums as he opens a packet that says 'Calm Cookies'. They are the same ones he offered Penny at her job interview. 'Wait, why are you still here, Penny? You should go home.'

'Well . . . I was just . . . Since you're still here . . .'

'Oh, no. I'm kind of already off,' DallerGut says, ambiguously.

'Pardon?'

'I actually live in the attic of this building. It's been remodelled for my use.'

'Oh . . .'

Jingle.

The doorbell rings, and in comes an elderly customer.

'I'm sorry, we're out of stock today,' says Penny, but DallerGut steps in, signalling for Penny to wait as he walks forward.

'Actually, I'm not here to buy anything. Do you take pre-orders?' the customer asks.

'Of course, please come over here.' DallerGut deftly hides the cookie behind his back and welcomes the customer in, followed by a couple more. All are of different ages and genders, but their eyes are all swollen. They must have cried before going to sleep.

'Something must've happened to them,' Penny whispers to DallerGut, making sure her voice is inaudible to the customers.

'Looks like it. I know them all. They're actually here later than usual.'

'They must've tossed and turned before falling asleep.'

'Quite possibly.'

DallerGut takes them to the staff lounge to the right of the entrance. Penny follows, which DallerGut does not seem to mind.

Reached through a creaky arch-shaped door, the lounge reveals itself to be quite expansive. A chandelier that looks more like a small lamp gives off a warm, cosy feel. There are ragged, patched-up cushions, a couch and a long table made from a single piece of wood. The lounge feels complete, with an old fridge, a coffee machine and a snack basket.

The customers sit as DallerGut grabs a handful of candies from the snack basket and starts handing them out. 'This is called Deep Sleep Candy. Sweet and effective. Perfect for sleepless nights like tonight.'

They take the candies one by one. Then suddenly, tears start streaming down their faces.

'I'm sorry, I should've given you Calm Cookies first,' says DallerGut. 'But no worries. You can cry all you want. Whatever happens here stays here. Now, what dream shall I prepare for you?'

'I broke up with my partner a few days ago.' A young woman sitting by the entrance opens up first. 'I've been okay, coping with it well, but today I had a sudden migraine, and my heart was burning like crazy. I don't feel lonely, but I just feel miserable. Ever since the break-up, I can't seem to move on, not even one step. I want to know what's on my mind, whether it is regret or resentment. Will I understand if I see him again in my dream?'

'I lost my older sister when I was little. We had a big age gap. And yesterday was my twenty-fifth birthday. The same age my sister was when she passed away. It dawns on me just how young she was when she left, and it aches. I would love to see her, at least in my dreams, and, like, have a chat. Do you think she's doing okay?'

'The contest deadline is coming up soon, but I still have no idea what to submit. Everyone else seems to have brilliant, inspirational ideas, and I feel so dumb. I'm getting old, and there are no other skills that I've mastered, and I can't seem to give up on my dream and what I want to do.'

'I turned seventy last month. It's been a long, full life. I was packing to move into a new home today and came across some pictures of myself from my student days, and of my wedding. And those old memories have been haunting me all day. Then, as I lay in bed, sorrow crept over me. The time that had flown by felt so cruel.'

The customers all have their own stories to tell, and it takes a long while, as DallerGut takes thorough notes. 'Thank you, everyone,' he says eventually. 'Your pre-order applications are all filled out. We will start preparing your dreams.'

The customers stand up from their seats as they finish the Deep Sleep Candy.

'When can we expect to receive our dreams?' asks the old lady, who is the last one to stand up.

'Let me see . . . For some of you, I can get them right away, but the rest of you may have to wait a bit longer.'

'How long?'

'I can't be sure enough to tell you right now, but there is one thing you all need to do in order to receive your dreams intact.'

'What is it?'

'You must try to get a deep sleep every night. That's all.'

The customers finally leave the store. Standing next to DallerGut, who is busy compiling all the notes, Penny gets ready to take off.

'Do you sell these kinds of made-to-order dreams often?' she asks.

'Not too often, but sometimes. I always find it more rewarding than selling pre-made dreams. You will understand when you run a store for a long time like me. Now, off you go.'

'Okay.'

The Eyelid Scales continue moving up and down.

'Oh, Penny, wait!' DallerGut stops Penny, who is about to leave.

'Yes?'

'I forgot to give you an official welcome. Congratulations! We're happy to have you work with us. Hope you like it here so far.'

Miye Lee was born in Busan in 1990. After graduating from the Busan National University School of Materials Science and Engineering, she worked as a semiconductor engineer at Samsung Electronics. Her debut novel *DallerGut Dream Department Store* was published in Korea in 2020, and entirely funded through enthusiastic fan response on a popular crowdfunding service. The duology has since become a global bestseller and has been published in over eighteen languages. Her latest work is a novella titled *Break Room*.

Sandy Joosun Lee is a translator and interpreter based in Seoul. Her translations include Won-pyung Sohn's *Almond* (HarperVia, 2020). She also works in animation, translating and developing animated content, which includes *The Witcher: Nightmare of the Wolf* (2021) and *Star Wars: Visions* (2023).